DANDE

Veronica Bennett works part-time as a
English lecturer. She began her writing career
as a freelance journalist, but soon moved into
fiction. Her first book, *Monkey*, was
published in 1998 and was acclaimed by *The
Times Educational Supplement* as "an
impressively well-written and audacious
debut". Amongst her other titles for Walker
are *The Boy-free Zone* and *Fish Feet*.
Veronica Bennett is married to a university
professor and has two children.

Books by the same author

The Boy-free Zone

Fish Feet

Monkey

DANDELION AND BOBCAT

VERONICA BENNETT

WALKER BOOKS
AND SUBSIDIARIES
LONDON • BOSTON • SYDNEY

First published 2000 by Walker Books Ltd
87 Vauxhall Walk, London SE11 5HJ

This edition published 2001

2 4 6 8 10 9 7 5 3

Text © 2000 Veronica Bennett
Cover Illustration © 2000 Nick Sharratt

This book has been typeset in Sabon

Printed and bound in Great Britain by
Cox & Wyman Ltd, Reading, Berkshire

British Library Cataloguing in Publication Data:
a catalogue record for this book
is available from the British Library

ISBN 0-7445-7899-X

CONTENTS

BOBCAT AND THE FEEBLE FAIRY STORY

Bobcat couldn't believe it. He'd assumed Dandelion was a nickname, like Bobcat. But Dandelion's name really *was* Dandelion.

"What have we here?" Sir looked doubtfully at the last name on the register. "A weed in the garden this morning?"

"Well, *I* weed in the bathroom this morning," said Dandelion, looking at her fingernails.

Several girls gasped. Bobcat's legs went rigid. His bottom superglued itself to his chair.

"And another thing," added Dandelion. Calmly she surveyed the class. "If anyone here wants me to beat them up, they just need to say that picking a dandelion makes you wet the bed." Her eyes rolled exaggeratedly. "What a great joke! I've never heard *that* one before!"

There was a blank moment of disbelief, then a riot broke out in the classroom. Sir was too astonished to stand on his chair and drop the *Children's Encyclopedia of Plants and Animals* onto his desk, which was how he usually stopped riots. Mrs Goodman, the head teacher, flung the door open and pointed her ballpoint pen menacingly at the class, her eyebrows twitching. She shut the door on a pin-drop silence.

"Dandelion..." Sir glanced at the register again. "Dandelion Primrose Gardener, stand up."

Dandelion stood up.

Her looks, decided Bobcat, were even odder than her name. Her hair stuck out all round her head like candy floss, as yellowy-orange as the petals of a dandelion. She had large eyes set in pale skin, with freckles sprinkled over her nose like hundreds and thousands.

And what a nose! Bobcat had heard of turned-up noses, though he wasn't sure he'd ever actually seen one until he saw Dandelion's. It was definitely turned up, but it was pointed, so that from the side it looked like a dog's nose, with the nostrils facing outwards. On Saturday, when Dandelion had first arrived, Bobcat had kept looking at it, and looking away, and looking at it again.

"Are you aware of how rude you've just been?" asked Sir in his you-ain't-seen-nothin'-yet voice.

"Yes," replied Dandelion calmly, "but you

were rude first." Her voice was strange, too. High-pitched, like the cries of tiny birds.

Sir couldn't deny this. He opened his mouth, but no words came out. The silence in the room was as thick as the strawberry syrup Bobcat had watched Dandelion squeeze all over her cereal that morning.

Dandelion seemed pleased. She smiled down at the horrified faces. "Well, he was, wasn't he?"

No one had the courage to look at her. Instead they looked at Bobcat. Silent laughter was brimming out of Joe's eyes. Ollie had clamped his hands together as if praying to be transported somewhere else. It was very hot in the classroom. Bobcat could feel sweat gathering where his hair came out of his head.

"Dandelion Primrose Gardener," barked Sir again. "You will stay after school tomorrow and every day this week and do a task I set you. We obviously need to begin your education as soon as possible." He softened his voice and addressed the whole class. "Wouldn't you agree that this dandelion needs *taming*?"

No one spoke.

Sir sat down on the corner of his desk, adjusting his glasses. "Now, Year Six, let's get on. New term, new reader. Robert Catterick, give out these books."

Bobcat slopped reading-books down on

tables, aware of the awestruck atmosphere around him. Concentrating hard, he rehearsed answers to the questions he knew they'd chuck at him later.

No, she's not related to me. I never saw her until Saturday.

No, I had no idea she was going to say that. If I had, I'd have stuffed the blackboard duster in her mouth.

Yes, I know she looks strange, but she can't help that.

No, for the twentieth time, she's not my sister. Lizzie's my sister. Dandelion's my foster-sister.

A foster-sister is someone who lives with you because she can't live with her proper parents for a while.

He couldn't tell them why his parents had agreed to take on Dandelion, or where her real parents were, though. The truth was, he didn't know.

At lunchtime Bobcat collected his football from the cloakroom and ran onto the field.

"Where did your mum and dad dig her up from?" asked Joe, jerking his thumb towards Dandelion, who was surrounded by girls. "Sorry, I didn't mean—"

"Social services," said Bobcat.

"You're a lying git, Catterick," said Ollie. He jumped up and down like footballers on

TV, doing his warming-up exercises. "Sisters don't come from social services. When my mum got my sister she went to a hospital."

Joe took off his spectacles, put them in their case and put the case solemnly in his pocket. "Your sister was a baby, Ollie," he explained. "But Dandelion's eleven."

"You two think you're so clever," accused Ollie, still suspicious. "But I bet you know poo-all about where babies really come from."

Bobcat sighed. "Dandelion's not an ordinary sister—"

"You can say that again!" interrupted Ollie.

"—she's a foster-sister. She's living with my family because her own parents can't look after her for a while." He couldn't resist showing off a little. "My mum and dad are acting *in loco parentis*."

"They're nuts, you mean?" asked Ollie.

Joe raised his eyebrows. "Loco what did you say?"

"*In loco parentis*," repeated Bobcat patiently. "It's Latin."

"See?" said Ollie to Joe, with triumph. "Everyone knows loco means nuts."

Joe, who went to the library a lot, considered. "It's that Roman sport, isn't it? They used to throw lunatics to the lions, or something, didn't they?"

Bobcat tossed the football a couple of times, then dropped it and put his foot on it. "I think they threw Christians to the lions, Joe. Not lunatics. Though if Ollie had been around then..."

Ollie tried an illegal tackle, but Bobcat got out of the way. "My dad says *in loco parentis* means 'in place of the parents'," he explained. "It's like sending on a substitute."

"Did the lions eat the Christians alive, then?" asked Ollie.

Joe went to push up his glasses, which he always did when he was thinking. Then he remembered they weren't there, and pretended he needed to scratch his nose. "But why are your parents coming on as substitute parents for Dandelion," he asked, "when they've got you and Lizzie already? I mean, they're hardly sitting on the bench, are they? They're in the starting line-up!"

"What are you talking about?" asked Ollie, frowning. "Parents don't play football." He paused doubtfully, looking at Bobcat side-ways. "Do they?"

"It's all right, Ol," said Bobcat. "Joe's only trying to be clever."

"Me! *You* started it, like you—"

"Look, they're doing it for money," interrupted Bobcat. "Social services are going to pay them."

You're going to have a new sister, Mum had said. Not a sleepy baby like Lizzie was, but a ready-made sister of your own age to play with.

Bobcat had tried to tell her that boys of his age didn't play with girls. They didn't take any notice of their *real* sister, let alone a fostered one. How could she seriously expect Robert Catterick, the best striker Kneshworth Juniors had ever seen, and undisputed king of "the Sixers", as Year Six liked to call themselves, to walk into school on the first day of the summer term with a *girl*? And not just any old girl, but the funniest-looking girl anyone had ever seen outside the pages of a comic?

Don't make that face, Robert, she'd said.

He had secretly decided that he would have to run away and seek his fortune, with his belongings tied up in the spotted cloth Mum used for cleaning the windows. But there had been take-away pizza and chocolate chip ice cream for tea on Saturday, and he'd decided running away was babyish.

"Come on, then, is anyone in goal?"

Joe kicked the ball from under Bobcat's foot and took up his penalty-shooting position. Every lunchtime they had a penalty shoot-out, with the three of them taking turns at being goalie, penalty-taker and referee. Then they sat down on a bench and ate their sandwiches. Then they kicked around the playground with the other boys until Joe's gadgety watch and Sir's whistle told them it was time to go in.

This afternoon all the benches were occupied, so Bobcat and Ollie and Joe sat down on the dusty grass at the edge of the field. Ollie kept bouncing the football on the playground tarmac. The sun was very hot. The final week of the Easter holidays had been gripped by a heat wave which showed no sign of relenting. Bobcat felt very sweaty.

"Balloon race was great on Saturday," said Ollie. He put down the football and opened a can of fizzy drink. "Weather was just right."

Disappointment surged through Bobcat's stomach. Every year he went to the balloon race with Ollie and Joe and Ollie's dad, who skippered a crew. This year he hadn't been able to go because Saturday was the day Dandelion had arrived.

"Don't talk about it," he said to Ollie. "I had to stay in all day waiting to say hello to my precious new sister. And then she was so late I could have gone to the balloon race anyway."

"Pleased to meet you, Robert darling!" said Ollie in a high-pitched voice, leaping to his feet and spreading his arms. Lemonade splashed onto the grass. "Did she give you a kiss?"

"I'll give *you* a kiss in a minute," threatened Bobcat. Ollie grinned, but put the drink to his lips just in case.

Bobcat thought about the miraculous sight of the balloons filling and rising and plucking their baskets from the ground, and soaring away, travelling with the wind until the horizon came up to meet them. And he had missed it all for a foster-sister he hadn't even wanted in the first place.

A lot of people had collected around Dandelion, eager to meet the heroine whose first encounter with Sir had been so fearless. In the midst of their chatter, Bobcat heard his own name.

"Why are you living at Catterick's?"

Samantha Pilkington, the most popular girl in the class, pushed to the front of the crowd. She offered Dandelion a crisp. Dandelion took one.

"Here, take the whole pack," urged Samantha, smiling.

Dandelion took it. "I'm living there because I can't live with my mother."

"Why not?"

Those nearest to Dandelion were all girls. Bobcat, with Ollie and Joe and the other boys, was further away but within earshot. No one talked much. They even munched and slurped quietly. They all wanted to hear what Dandelion would say.

"I'm not sure if I should tell you."

"Why not?" repeated Samantha.

"Oh … I don't want to put her in danger. You know."

They didn't know. There was a baffled silence. Bobcat began to feel uneasy.

"Well, it all started a long time ago. Before

15

I was born." She nibbled a crisp. "My mother made some enemies, you see, and now they're after her. In fact..." She paused, bowing her head. "In fact, they've captured her, and put her in prison."

Bobcat felt like sicking up his peanut butter sandwich. What a liar! And what sort of feeble fairy story was this? He wouldn't stand for it. Before he could change his mind he had invaded the circle of girls. "Dandelion!"

"Shut up and go away, Catterick," said Samantha Pilkington. "We want to hear about Dandelion's mother."

"But what she's telling you isn't true!" protested Bobcat.

Dandelion glared at him. "What *is* true, then?"

Bobcat didn't know. And he couldn't invent something, after accusing Dandelion of doing exactly that.

"I don't know," he confessed. "But I *do* know you're making all this up."

Her eyes got larger. The whites looked blue, with tiny veins running through them. The light reflected from the sun-struck playground made her face look very pale.

"I'm *not* making it up. What do you know about it? Your mother's just ordinary. But mine..." Her head drooped again, her face disappearing into the dandelion hair. "Mine's a princess."

16

They were astonished. Some girls gasped. But Samantha Pilkington tossed her head scornfully. "Of course she is!" She leaned towards Dandelion. "Princess who, then? Of what country, then?"

Dandelion's pond-water-coloured eyes turned to her. "Her name is Azalea, Crown Princess of Harmon Major and All Its Dominions. What happened was…" She stopped, and shook her head impatiently. "Anyway, she should be queen, but she isn't. One day she will be, though. And then what do you think will happen?"

"What?" asked Samantha, in a fainter voice.

Dandelion's eyes didn't look like pond water any more. They gleamed. "I – *I* – will be Dandelion Primrose, Crown Princess of Harmon Major and All Its Dominions!"

There was a pause, and then, just as if they'd rehearsed it, everyone started to laugh. Ollie and Joe laughed too. But Bobcat couldn't. He was disgusted, and crosser with Dandelion than he could explain.

"You're pathetic," he told her coldly. "Don't you know what a fool you're making of yourself?"

The whistle blew. Dandelion's audience began to drift away.

"No, *you're* the fool, Bobcat," she said. "For not believing me."

The next morning the heat wave was worse. Mrs Goodman stood on the little raised platform in the hall, reading the notices at the end of assembly. She was wearing a sleeveless dress. When she moved, her arms wobbled like cold custard.

"The Kneshworth Bash and Ball will take place on the first Saturday of half-term, on the school field!" she declared sternly. As always, she had a ballpoint pen stuck behind her ear. "There will be lots of special attractions, and we're all going to have a great time and raise more money than ever before, aren't we!"

The school droned the obligatory cheer. Dandelion took advantage of the noise to lean across and whisper to Bobcat. "What's the Kneshworth Bash and Ball?"

"It's like a big party," he explained. "There's a parade through the village, with a carnival princess, and a dance in the evening."

"Can I be the carnival princess?" she asked eagerly.

"I doubt it. Everyone will vote for Samantha Pilkington."

"Why?"

"Because they're too scared not to."

"But that's not fair!"

Bobcat didn't care. The village of Kneshworth's annual day of jollity had been part of his life for so long he couldn't find any enthusiasm for the carnival princess or anything else. It was for little kids and girls. Why couldn't the village organize a five-a-side tournament instead? Or a roller-blading competition? Or, better still, an assault course, with rope ladders and tunnels?

Mrs Goodman rapped her pen on the overhead projector. "And you all know what's happening on Friday week, don't you?"

Silence. They didn't.

"First cricket fixture, against St Barnabas!"

A long, throaty cheer, with some whooping from the back where the Sixers stood, flowed through the hall. St Barnabas were the worst cricketers in the Spenmouth Schools League. They were the worst footballers, too, and had been thrashed twelve–nil by Kneshworth (double hat-trick by R. Catterick, Capt., duly reported in the *Advertiser*). Now that the football season was over, cricket waited with its own glories in store. Bobcat smiled with satisfaction. By Jupiter, as Dad would say, he couldn't wait to get his hands on that bat.

As they jostled down the corridor to the classroom, Ollie appeared at his elbow. "How's life with the lion?" He grinned.

"All right."

"Is she as daft at home as she is at school?"

Not far off, Bobcat wanted to say. But he decided not to. She'd only arrived three days ago, but he'd already noticed that when she was awkward Mum and Dad didn't tell her off, but reasoned with her instead. And when she did stupid things, like deliberately upsetting Dad's CD collection all over the floor, or making a snowstorm in the bathroom with the talcum powder, they took no notice, and wouldn't let Bobcat interfere. Mum cuddled her a lot too, when she had time off from cuddling Lizzie.

The noise in the classroom was louder than the usual Sir-free commotion. When Bobcat opened the door he wasn't very surprised to see Dandelion kneeling up on a chair, grasping its back and shouting. But he *was* surprised that the person shouting back at her was Joe.

"Don't talk such total rubbish, you … you … *girl*!" he taunted. "You don't know anything!"

Dandelion's cheeks were bright red. "I do so! I know they're going to lose!"

Bobcat realized they were arguing about St Barnabas. But why was Joe saying they were going to win? And what did Dandelion, who had never heard of St Barnabas until ten minutes ago, know about it?

"Shut up, Dandelion," he said. "Everyone knows St Barnabas are going to lose. They always do."

Joe pulled Bobcat's shirt, spinning him round so hard that both boys almost lost their balance. "It's not St Barnabas, you dipstick!

She says United are going to lose the Cup Final!" He was furious. "Three–two to Liverpool, she says!"

"*What?*"

Making up a story about an imprisoned princess was stupid enough, but at least it was girls' stuff. Venturing onto boys' turf was much, much stupider. Bobcat jeered louder than the others. He even pushed Dandelion's shoulder, making her sway backwards. But she kept her balance on the chair, kneeling up so tall that she towered over them. Her face didn't crumple. In fact, Bobcat thought he'd never seen anyone's face look less like crumpling.

"What's your score prediction, then?" she asked Joe defiantly.

Joe had relaxed. He knew he had everyone's support. He sat on a table so that his eyes were level with hers. "Two–one." He grinned. "To *United*, of course."

Dandelion was calm. "All right, then, I'll make a bargain with you." Bobcat could see that she was grasping the back of the chair very tightly, perhaps in case someone pushed her off it. "If you're brave enough to take it on."

"Go on, then," challenged Joe, bright-eyed.

"If Liverpool win three–two, you've got to turn up at the Kneshworth Bash in Liverpool strip ..."

The whole class gasped. "Liverpool strip?"

echoed Joe weakly.

"... and wear it the whole afternoon. People can sponsor you, for charity. Why not? And if United win two–one, you can decide what you want *me* to do for charity. I don't mind how silly it is!"

A crafty look came over Joe's face. "I name it, you'll do it?"

"Of course." She got down from the chair and sat on it, turning her back to him. "You'd better start thinking of something, hadn't you? Since you're so sure United are going to win."

Bobcat began to look forward to Dandelion's embarrassing appearance at the Kneshworth Bash. It would be worth every penny he'd sponsor her for, and serve her right.

"You're on, then, *girl*," said Joe. He took off his glasses, wiped them on his trousers and put them on again. His face was pink, but he was smiling. "And don't worry, I'll think of something *incredibly* silly."

Dandelion still had her back to him. People were sitting down and getting pencil-cases out. The show was over. "I certainly won't worry," she murmured.

Bobcat couldn't resist. "You may need to, weed-face," he said unkindly.

"Shut up!" Her eyes looked wild. "And you'd better stop laughing, because you're going to lose that crummy cricket match too, Captain Catterick!"

DANDELION AND THE SIGN OF THE SPIDER

The tasks Sir set Dandelion to do after school each day that week weren't very hard. On Wednesday she had to put away all the books people had left out in the school library.

"Call this a library?" she said scornfully to Bobcat when Sir had closed the door. "It's more like a cupboard! At my last school we had a proper library."

Bobcat didn't ask where her last school was. It was bad enough that Mum had insisted he stay behind with Dandelion while she took Lizzie shopping in Spenmouth, without having to listen to more nonsense about Harmon Major and All Its Dominions. He sat down at one of the two computers and started it up.

"Where does a book about dinosaurs go?" asked Dandelion.

"Er…" Bobcat wasn't listening very

carefully. "With the other books about dinosaurs?"

He studied the computer screen. What could he waste time doing until Dandelion was ready? Drawing? He clicked into the artwork program and began to draw a zebra.

"But where are they?" asked Dandelion plaintively. "I can't do this. You'll have to help me."

Bobcat pretended he hadn't heard. Artistically, he turned the blue and yellow stripes on his zebra pink and green. But his silence only made Dandelion more determined to disturb him.

"*Please!*" she pleaded, sitting down on the other computer chair. "If you don't help me we'll be here for ever."

Bobcat's watch said ten to four. Mum had told them to be home by half past. He looked at the pile of books on the table. It was a ten-minute job. But he knew by now – and so did everyone else at school – that Dandelion would make as much fuss as possible about anything, however simple.

"Look," he said impatiently, "it's easy. You look at the book, then you look on the shelf for the same subject, and put it there in alphabetical order of the author's name. Didn't they teach you anything at your last school?"

He knew this was an unkind swipe, but he couldn't help it. Sitting there with her finger in her mouth and her shoulders hunched, she just looked so … annoying.

"What about stories?" She put down the dinosaur book and picked up *James and the Giant Peach*. "Where do they go?"

"Dandelion…"

"You've got to be nice to me, I'm your sister."

"You're *not* my sister." He turned back to the computer and frowned at the zebra for a moment. Then, because he wanted his tea, he relented. "All right, I'll tell you where each book goes, and you put it away. Can you do that, do you think?"

"Oh, thanks!"

They made slow progress. Dandelion kept opening the books and reading bits out, and forgetting where Bobcat had told her to put them. After he had put a yellow mane and tail on the zebra, then given it wings, then deleted the wings, he began to get bored.

"What's next?" Glancing very briefly at the book she was holding out, he deleted the zebra and drew a spider, giving it hairy legs and, for good measure, green eyes. "That one goes over there in the corner with the history books."

Dandelion didn't move.

"Dandelion, are you listening?"

She put the book back on the table. She was staring at the screen with her mouth open.

"Of course!" she cried, clutching Bobcat's shoulder. "Of *course*!"

Bobcat tried to wriggle away from her, but she gripped tighter. Her nails dug into him through his shirt. "Bobcat – what have you done?"

"Er…" Bobcat was unwilling to admit he didn't know what she was getting so excited about. "I've drawn a spider, stupid," he said crossly. "Can't you see it?"

She sat down carefully in the other computer chair, her eyes fixed on the screen. "It's not just a *spider*, though – stupid – it's a tarantula." Her eyes flashed suddenly. "Can you save this drawing, and call it up any time you want?"

"Of course I can, stu—"

"Bobcat, neither of us is stupid, so just stop saying it. Save the tarantula, because we're going to need it again."

"What are you talking about?"

"Shut up and save the drawing!" She shook him by the shoulder.

"Let go of me, will you?" snapped Bobcat. But he did what she asked.

"Now type in 'Tarantula'," she instructed. "If you can spell it, that is."

"Of course I can spell it."

He expected nothing to happen, as no word processing program had been selected. But something *did* happen. The tarantula began to wave its legs menacingly. Its little eyes gleamed at Bobcat.

Dandelion clapped her hands. She let out a little yelp of joy. "Oh, how wonderful! I was right!"

"It's some sort of game, is it?" asked Bobcat. He was baffled by what the computer had done, but felt unwilling to admit it. Especially to a girl.

"No, it's not a game, silly. Don't you see? The spider you drew was a sign."

Bobcat was getting exasperated. "Why don't you say something sensible sometimes?"

"It was a sign that you've been chosen." She leaned towards him. "*You* are the only one who can find the clues."

"What clues?"

"The clues that will lead me to my mother."

His exasperation burst out. "But it's all rubbish! It's just a stupid story!"

"It is *not*!" she squeaked impatiently. "Listen…"

Bobcat refused to listen. He put his hands over his ears. But Dandelion took his hands away and held them in hers.

"Look. Everyone in Harmon Major knows that Tarantula is very powerful, and that he'll only help you if you're clever enough. He knows how I can get back to my mother, but he's locked the clues inside the computer."

Bobcat was listening despite himself.

Frowning, he waited for her to go on.

"I knew the key had to be something to do with a tarantula – a word, or a picture, or something. I've tried and tried to find the way in, but I've never been able to." She wriggled in her chair, and squeezed his hands more tightly. "When you drew that tarantula, I suddenly realized that the person with the power to make the clues appear isn't me at all, Bobcat. It's you."

Bobcat stared at her. He could tell that she believed what she was saying. Helplessly, he turned back to the computer. The spider on the screen was still waving its legs. He watched it for a moment. "What do I do now?"

"We need the password."

"What password?"

Dandelion let go of his hands. "Look, this is how it works. One clue leads to another, and the final clue will lead me back to my mother. The answer to each clue is the password to the next. But without the first password I can't find the first clue."

"So what's the first password, then?" he asked.

"Well … I don't know." She sat back despondently. Then the glow of a bright idea spread over her face, and she sat forward again. "But … oh, of course! *You* do!"

She clutched his arm. "Don't you think the first password might be something to do with *you*? Since you're the only one who can make it work?"

They looked at each other.

"Go on," she urged. "Type in your name or something."

Bobcat typed **ROBERT**. Nothing happened. Then he typed **CATTERICK**.

Again, nothing. Then he deleted both words and typed **BOBCAT**. Dandelion held her breath.

Nothing.

"It must be, it just *must* be you," murmured Dandelion. "Do you have any other names? A middle name, or another nickname? Does anyone call you anything special? Oh, think!"

Bobcat thought. "Well, sometimes … though I don't really like it … I get called King of the Sixers. Not because I want to be, but—"

Dandelion clutched his arm. "That's it! Tarantula is powerful, but who could be more powerful than a king! Try it!"

Bobcat typed **KING**.

"**Press Enter**" said the screen.

He hesitated, then pressed the Enter key.

The screen exploded into light. Instinctively Bobcat put his hands over his eyes.

"Tell us, Tarantula!" whispered Dandelion urgently. "Tell us the clue!"

The screen went black. Then some words appeared, arranged like a poem:

One on one, ten plus one,
Faster than a shot from a gun.
Thrice will chime the sound of a bell,
Then you'll face a bat out of hell.

Bobcat stared.

"Can you print it out?" asked Dandelion.

His finger shook as he pressed the button to start the printer. "What does it mean?"

"How slow you are!" She squatted impatiently beside the printer. "And how slow this machine is!"

"But what does it *mean*?" he repeated.

"That's what we've got to find out. At last!" She pulled at the print-out, almost ripping it. "Now we've got the first clue, nothing can stop me getting back to her!" She gazed up at him, grinning. "Thank you – oh, *thank* you, King Bobcat!"

Bobcat's mum was French. She'd been a translator before Bobcat and Lizzie were born, and still worked sometimes for her old firm, when they had too much translating to do. Heavy envelopes of English papers would arrive, and Mum would shut herself in the dining-room after Lizzie was in bed and produce heavy envelopes of French papers.

"Dandelion's been telling everyone at school that her mother's a princess," said

Bobcat when he looked into the dining-room that evening to say goodnight. Dandelion had already gone upstairs, and was splashing in the bathroom.

Mum looked up calmly. The desk lamp shone on her papers. "And do they believe her?"

"No, of course not. They're laughing themselves totally sick."

She studied his face. "Which is embarrassing for you, I think?"

"You could say that. Why does she have to tell such stupid lies?"

Mum sighed. She put down her pen and rubbed her hands over her face, making her hair stand up in little wisps.

"And she's horrible, too," added Bobcat.

"*Horrible?*" Mum took her hands away from her face. Bobcat almost smiled at the way her French accent made the word sound.

"Well, she's so … show-offy. She wants to be the leader all the time." He stopped and thought. "And she's selfish. You know the way she took the biggest slice of cake at teatime? Well, on Monday she took Samantha Pilkington's whole packet of crisps without thanking her. And she talks about herself all the time."

Mum was listening with interest. Bobcat got into his stride.

"She says that her mother's been imprisoned

by her enemies. She says she's going to rescue her, and restore the rightful heiress to the throne."

There was a pause. Bobcat scratched his ankle where his sock dug in and made little grooves.

"It sounds as if she's read a lot of stories," said Mum thoughtfully. "Did she say which country her mother was imprisoned in?"

"It's just a made-up country, Mum." He pretended he couldn't remember its name. "You know, like Transylvania or something. Hughey Smith believes her – he says there are loads of places in Europe we never hear about – but he's such a dipstick he'd believe anything."

"Transylvania's a real place. Do you remember Miss Waller?"

Bobcat considered. "That dolled-up blonde with the briefcase? She's the social services lady, isn't she?"

"That's right." Mum was amused, but tried not to let him see. "She told us what she knows about Dandelion's background. It isn't much, I'm afraid. But I don't think there's a princess in it!"

Bobcat asked the question he'd been bursting with since he entered the room. "Her mother isn't really in prison, is she? Here, in England, I mean?"

"No."

"Is her dad in prison?"

"No."

"Promise?"

"Promise."

"Where *is* her mother, then?"

"She's…" Mum thought for a bit. "It's impossible for her to be with Dandelion at present, that's all. But it's only for—"

She was stopped by a scream from upstairs, followed by a thud. Bobcat heard scampering noises and raised voices. He dashed into the hall. Dad's legs were disappearing round the corner at the top of the staircase. Racing after them, Bobcat got to the door of Dandelion's room just in time to see gentle, long-haired, guitar-playing Dad gather Dandelion's bloom of hair in one hand and Lizzie's ponytail in the other, and wrench the two girls apart.

"I will *not* have fighting in this house!" he bellowed.

Even Bobcat, who hadn't done anything, was scared. Dad didn't have many rules, but the No Fighting rule was law. It had been explained to Dandelion when she'd arrived on Saturday, along with the No Football in the House rule and the No Tormenting Garden Creatures rule.

Lizzie was scared too. But Dandelion showed no fear. She kicked out at Dad's shins, making him dance from foot to foot like a string puppet. Red-faced, spluttering with fury, she didn't notice that the more she fought his grasp the tighter it got.

"Let me go, let me *go*!" shrieked Dandelion. "Let me at her – I want to kill her!"

Dad had dropped Lizzie's ponytail. She tried to flee to her own bedroom, but Bobcat caught her. She was only six, and very skinny, and he did it easily. While she struggled in his arms he could feel her tears on his own cheeks. "Calm down, will you, Liz?" he urged.

But she couldn't hear him above the noise Dandelion was making.

"Kill her, kill her!" The baby-bird voice had turned into the rasping screech of a hawk. Dad had grabbed her by the arms, and was trying to cuddle her against his chest, but she kept twisting her body away from him.

"She's hysterical," he muttered breathlessly. "By Jupiter, Bob, she's stronger than me."

At that moment, Mum arrived. "What on earth—"

"Get rid of Lizzie, will you, Paul?" Dad said it like an instruction, not a request. Mum's name was Marie-Paul, but Dad had lost the Marie years ago. Bobcat often wished he'd lost the Paul instead.

"What's the matter with Dandelion?" he asked, more puzzled now than scared.

Mum's face asked Dad the same question, but she gathered Lizzie up, making soothing noises in the back of her throat, and took her away without a word.

Dandelion's strength faltered at last. She sat down heavily on the floor, her face peering tearfully from under the umbrella of hair. "I hate her, I *hate* her," she murmured. Her wide, wet eyes looked up imploringly at Bobcat's dad. "How *dare* she?"

"What's she done?" asked Bobcat.

Dandelion twisted the hem of her pyjama jacket round her fingers, screwing it into a knot. "I was in the bathroom," she began miserably, "and when I came back she was in here, lying on my bed."

"That was naughty of her," said Dad.

"Naughty of her! She hates me!" cried Dandelion.

"Of course she doesn't—"

"She *must* hate me!" She was almost crying again. She went to the bed and picked up something from the pillow. "Look!"

Dad and Bobcat looked. It was a drawing, on a sheet of the scrap paper Mum gave Lizzie for scribbling. It was a six-year-old's attempt to draw a dandelion, with a crayoned-in stem and petals drawn with a yellow highlighter pen. Beside the dandelion, mysteriously, was the crude drawing of a bed.

"Go on, laugh!" shouted Dandelion. Her rage burst out again so suddenly that Bobcat jumped. "Let's all have a good laugh about my funny name, shall we?"

Mum had come back from Lizzie's room, looking upset. She put her arms round Dandelion. "Lizzie just wanted to give you something she'd made," she explained. "She drew you, and your bed beside you, to show she's glad to have you staying here with us. She thought it would make you happy. She doesn't understand."

Dandelion cried some more, into the front of Mum's T-shirt. "But *you* understand, don't you?" she blurted out between sobs.

"Of course."

"Oh…" Bobcat understood too. On her first morning Dandelion had threatened to beat up any thoughtless clever-clogs who might be thinking of making the joke about picking a dandelion and wetting the bed.

With a sigh, Dad sat down on Dandelion's bedroom chair. He put his hair behind his ears and looked solemnly at the drawing. "Poor old Lizzie," he said softly. "The joke's on her. *She's* the one who wets her bed."

"*I'm* the one that gets teased about it, though!" sniffed Dandelion.

Dad gave her a sympathetic look. Then something seemed to amuse him, and his mouth twitched. He cuffed Bobcat's shoulder gently. "Hey, Bob, it's a good job you don't learn French at your school…"

"Why?" asked Bobcat.

"Well, in French that superstition about

dandelions is part of the actual language. Only don't let anyone at school know, or Dandelion's life really *will* be a misery." Glancing at Mum, he folded the drawing and put it in his trouser pocket. "Tell him, Paul."

She was still stroking Dandelion's hair. "The French word for dandelion is *pissenlit*," she said to Bobcat. "Literally, 'pee in bed'."

BOBCAT AND THE BAT OUT OF HELL

Joe and Bobcat gazed glumly at the rain running down Bobcat's bedroom window. "The trouble is," pondered a worried-looking Joe, "you don't expect this sort of weather so late in the season, do you?"

The lawn was a patchwork of puddles held together with bits of grass. Water ran off the roof of the shed and collected in the shaped plastic seat of Lizzie's swing. The sky looked steel grey, with the clouds almost touching the rooftops.

"I mean," continued Joe, "supposing the Cup Final's rained off?"

There was a silence while they all considered this.

"You're hoping it *is* rained off, aren't you?" cried Ollie, who was sprawling on Bobcat's England flag duvet cover. He sat up. "Joe Whittle, you coward! You're scared of a *girl*!"

Swearing, Joe shoved Ollie so hard he almost fell off the bed. Bobcat came to the rescue. "If it's rained off, they'll just postpone it for a few days. It'll still take place before the Bash, so what difference will it make?"

"It might make a big difference to United," pointed out Joe. "They might be past their peak."

"Well, so might Liverpool," said Bobcat sensibly.

"I bet next Saturday will be the hottest Cup Final day since records began," declared Ollie. "I truly bet!"

Joe sat down on the edge of the bed. Then he jumped up again. "I've suddenly thought what I can get Dandelion to do at the Bash. It's *brilliant*!"

"When United win two–one!" shouted Ollie. "U–ni–*ted*, U–ni–*ted*, U–ni— "

"Shut up and listen," said Joe. He pushed up his spectacles. "Dandelion's a bit weird, isn't she?"

"A *bit* weird!" smiled Bobcat.

"And one of the weirdest things about her is her name, yes?"

"Ye–es." Bobcat wondered what was coming.

"Well, you know the Kneshworth Bash fancy dress competition?"

"Ye–es," said Bobcat again.

Joe was so excited that he laughed loudly.

"Listen to this! When Jenny was about ten she entered it – as a dandelion! And to make it funny, she had a baby's potty round her neck!"

They stared at him. Jenny was his fourteen-year-old sister.

"She didn't win, but I know where Mum keeps the costume. It'll fit Dandelion, won't it? And she'll have to wear it the whole afternoon. She can collect the sponsorship money in the potty!"

There was a silence. Bobcat felt uncomfortable. He wanted Dandelion to have to do something spectacularly silly as much as Joe and Ollie did. But they hadn't seen her scarlet-faced fury on Wednesday night.

"I'm not sure, Joe," he ventured.

"Why not?" Ollie's grin was nearly as wide as his face. "It's a great idea!"

"She's … a bit sensitive about her name. The way people go on about wetting the bed really upsets her."

"So?" said Joe, his eyes blank behind his glasses. "We want her to be upset, don't we? Anyone who talks the amount of nonsense she does deserves what they get."

Bobcat nibbled his thumbnail. He only did this when he was anxious. But why was he anxious? He took his thumb away from his mouth. "Look, Joe—"

The door opened. Dandelion stood there,

smiling broadly. In her hand was a small rolled-up blanket. "Look what I've got!"

"Can't you read the sign on the door?" asked Bobcat.

She took no notice. She unrolled the blanket on the floor. It was a thin pad with wires running through it like an electric blanket, attached to a little box. "Just watch this," she said happily. "It's amazing!"

The boys exchanged looks. "Where did you get that?" asked Bobcat. "And what is it, anyway?"

"Wait and see."

She ran into the bathroom. When she came back she was carrying a plastic tooth mug, half filled with water. She dipped her hand into it and flicked some water on the pad. All three boys jumped involuntarily as a loud buzzer sounded.

"See?" cried Dandelion excitedly. "The pad goes in Lizzie's bed, under the sheet. If it gets wet – you know, from wee – this little buzzer goes and Lizzie wakes up."

Bobcat was embarrassed. He hadn't told Joe and Ollie about the misunderstanding between Lizzie and Dandelion over the drawing, or that Lizzie wet her bed sometimes. Ollie could never be trusted with a secret. And although Mum was always saying it wasn't anything to make a fuss about, Bobcat didn't think small-minded types like Samantha

Pilkington would agree. He couldn't look at either of the boys, but heard their stifled giggling.

"What's the point in that?" he asked, frowning at Dandelion. "By that time she's already done it, so how does it stop her doing it?"

"Well, it doesn't, the first time," she admitted. "But slowly, the more often the buzzer wakes her just as she's *beginning* to wee, she'll learn to wake up in time to go to the bathroom without even getting a drop on the pad. It really works!"

"How do you know?" asked Joe, trying to keep his face serious. Ollie's chuckles escaped from behind the football magazine he was holding over his mouth.

"Because it worked for m— I mean, it's worked for other people. Lots of them."

"Let's try it!" Ollie's shrieks of laughter at last became uncontrollable. "Who's first? Go on, Bobcat!"

Dandelion whipped round. Her eyes looked like pebbles. "That's disgusting, you … you…" She couldn't think of a suitable insult. "When are you going to grow up?"

"Before you do!" screeched Ollie, wiggling his legs with glee.

Without warning, she threw the water from the tooth mug over his face. It splashed on his T-shirt and on Bobcat's football magazine.

"Hey!" yelled Bobcat. "You leave my friends alone!" Then he thought of something else. "And you can leave my sister alone, too!"

Dandelion stared at him, the empty mug in her hand.

"You think you're so clever, don't you?" Bobcat was spitting a little, without meaning to. "Showing off with your stupid gadget. Ollie was just being funny. Can't you take a joke?"

"So when do *you* ever do anything to help Lizzie?" she demanded.

"That's not the point." Something was strangling Bobcat. He felt like choking. "She's got Mum and Dad to look after her. She doesn't need anyone else fussing over her."

Ollie was drying his face on the corner of the England flag cover. "She's a nutcase," he told Joe.

"Oh, shut up." She gave Bobcat a hard look. "It's not fussing, it's helping. Mum says she needs—"

"And don't call her Mum!" shouted Bobcat. "She's not *your* mum, she's *my* mum! Call her Paul!"

Dandelion pushed back her fringe with stiff fingers. "I can't call her *Paul*, stupid!"

"Why not?"

"It's a man's name, stupid!"

"Stop calling me stupid!"

Joe butted in. "Ollie and I are going home.

43

Come on, Ol."

"What's my mum going to say about my T-shirt?" whined Ollie, getting off the bed. "It's soaked!"

"Look out of the window, Ollie," said Bobcat impatiently. "She'd be more surprised if you *weren't* wet."

Ollie shuffled sulkily across the room. "You're a git, Catterick."

When they'd gone, Dandelion bent down and rolled up the blanket with the little box inside. She put it under her arm. "Mum told me to call her Mum, so I will," she said sulkily. "And since my own mother is at this very moment being tortured in a tower, and I may never see her again, I think the least you could do is let me have a mother while I can."

She went out, leaving the door open. Bobcat shut it and sat down at his desk.

On the desk was the print-out of the clue from the computer. He read it through.

One on one, ten plus one,
Faster than a shot from a gun.
Thrice will chime the sound of a bell,
Then you'll face a bat out of hell.

What could *one on one* mean? Something standing on top of something else? *Ten plus one* obviously meant eleven, so did *one on one* mean two?

He was glad he hadn't told the others about the Tarantula game. Bobcat could do without their mockery. Joe was all right, but he did tend to think he knew everything. And the trouble was, Bobcat couldn't make up his own mind about the strange spider and the clues which were supposed to lead the way to Princess Azalea, Crown Princess of Harmon Major and All Its Dominions.

Dad had once said to him that in order to lie convincingly, you first have to know the truth. So was Dandelion lying in order to cover up the truth? Or was the story about the princess actually true? How could he know?

He looked more carefully at the clue. If he could solve it, it might prove beyond doubt that Dandelion was talking rubbish. Or it might not. Either way, he had to try.

The only thing he could find to write on was a school note he'd forgotten to give his parents. He turned the note over, took a pencil from his pocket and began to scribble. He wrote down one, and then one again. Eleven, not two. Then he wrote down ten and one. One hundred and one. Then he put them together. Eleven thousand one hundred and one. Then he wrote the number the other way. Ten thousand, one hundred and eleven.

And what about the rest of the rhyme?

Thrice meant three times, didn't it? A clock striking three? But what happened at three o'clock? It wasn't school letting-out time, and it wasn't teatime. It wasn't anything. And as for the bat out of hell ... what did bats have to do with anything? Were we talking vampires here? And didn't Dad sometimes play a song called "Bat Out of Hell" so loudly that he couldn't hear Mum shouting at him to turn it down? Could it be something to do with Dad's taste in rock music?

It was no use. It was giving him a headache. He put down the pencil. For lack of something else to do, he turned the note over and read it.

Kneshworth Junior School has been awarded a certificate by Spenmouth Council for the new playground mural. The certificate will be presented on Wednesday 22 May by Mr Alfred Winstanley, Leader of the Council, at 2.30 p.m.

Parents and friends are welcome to attend the ceremony, and take their children home straight afterwards.

Best wishes,
  M. Goodman.

He knew Mum and Dad couldn't go, but he'd better show them the note anyway. As he got up, the door opened. It was Lizzie.

"I've got a 'lectric thing to go in my bed," she announced.

"So you have," said Bobcat unenthusiastically. "Out of my way, child."

"I'm going to call it my Bizzie-Lizzie, 'cos it buzzes, and I'm Lizzie!" She followed him down the stairs. "It's the name of a flower, like Dandelion."

"It was Dandelion's idea, was it?" he asked.

"Course!"

It would be. He looked at Lizzie, who was swinging on the banister post. She looked very small. Yesterday she'd asked to play with the train set he hadn't touched for years, and he'd refused.

"Look, Liz," he said, "I'll just give this note to Mum, then we'll get the train set out, shall we?"

"Hats, boys!"

By Friday the weather had turned hot again. Sir strode between the players offering hats to those who hadn't got them. Ollie had forgotten his baseball cap and had to wear one of Sir's floppy cricket hats.

"Stylish!" teased Bobcat, dodging Ollie's swipes.

He felt great. They'd had some practice sessions in the nets and his bowling arm felt great. His batting wasn't bad either. Sir had muttered something about some lucky boys being all-rounders, and then pretended he'd been talking about something else. Sir never gave you compliments in case it made you big-headed.

This afternoon, Bobcat was sure even Sir would be pleased. As it was a home match, and Friday afternoon, Mrs Goodman had abandoned lessons. The whole school sprawled at the edge of the field. Bobcat could see Dandelion's orangey-yellow head beside Samantha Pilkington's blonde sheet of hair, captured, but untamed, by a blue headband.

They wouldn't watch any of the match, he knew. And even if they did, they wouldn't understand it. It was only two weeks since Dandelion had joined the school, but already she and Samantha seemed to be attracted to each other, and on the way to being best friends. Stranger friendships had been known, Bobcat supposed, but not many.

"Heads," he said.

It was tails. The St Barnabas captain, a wiry boy Bobcat had never seen before, grinned and announced his team would bat. "Then you'll know what you've got to beat," he said.

Bobcat smiled, and the boy shook his hand in a friendly enough way.

But that was where friendliness ended.

The St Barnabas team didn't look anything like the dismal lot who had trooped off the football field after their twelve–nil defeat by Kneshworth, only three months before. The truth began to seep through to Bobcat's stunned brain cells. They *weren't* the same lot. Neither the wiry boy nor most of the others had been in the football team. In fact, this wasn't just any old team. This was a *cricket* team.

Kneshworth was a small school in a village. But the trophies displayed in the cabinet outside Mrs Goodman's room proved they could win despite having to rely on the same few boys for both football and cricket. St Barnabas, however, was on the edge of Spenmouth, surrounded by a huge housing estate. Bobcat reckoned it must contain enough Year Six boys to make several football teams *and* a cricket team, but in the past had had no Sir and no enthusiasm. Clearly, all that had changed.

The teacher who came with them wasn't the usual fussing, breathless one. Bobcat hadn't noticed this when the team arrived. But now, as he waited nervously at the edge of the field, he looked more closely.

The teacher was definitely new. He was young, with a tracksuit and a whistle. He had done what someone at St Barnabas should have done ages ago. He had put the right boys into the right teams, and coached them, and made them believe, like Kneshworth, that they could win.

One useful St Barnabas batsman followed another. The runs piled up. It began to look as though Kneshworth might as well give up, when the batsman hit a high ball which came Bobcat's way. Bobcat reached for it, praying.

"*Fielded*, Catterick! Well *done*!"

Bobcat threw himself down on the grass, cradling the ball as if it were a precious ornament. The Kneshworth cheer was small. Despair had set in. When he was upright again he surveyed the scene carefully.

He *couldn't* let St Barnabas win. Not after twelve–nil, new teacher or no new teacher. And he couldn't let Dandelion's ridiculous prediction come true. He would just have to be a hero.

It was the end of the over. "I'll take the next one, shall I?" he asked Sir.

"Good idea," said Sir, without much enthusiasm. "I'm sure they've used up their best men by now, so you should thrash them."

He was wrong. In fact, he was dead wrong.

The next batsman was scary. The St Barnabas teacher had insisted on helmets, and the little cage over the boy's face made him look even scarier. He was so tall and strong that Bobcat wondered whether St Barnabas were illegally recruiting people's older brothers. Batsmen were supposed to be scared of *bowlers*. That was the reason for the helmets. But this boy squared up to Bobcat like a heavyweight boxer, planting the bat defiantly. Fear collected in Bobcat's legs.

Come on, Catterick, he told himself. What did Sir always say? Let the ball do the business.

He took his run and launched the ball. But the batsman sent it into orbit. People were actually shading their eyes from the sun and looking for it against the sky. And when it came down, there was no one there to catch it.

On the next ball Bobcat felt shaky, and bowled a no-ball.

"What's up, Catterick?" asked Sir quietly.

"I'm all right, Sir."

He bowled another ball. Again the batsman hit it beyond the boundary. As Bobcat walked back to start another run-up, the clock on the village church chimed three. They'd been playing for almost two hours, and still hadn't got them all out.

That was when it struck him. Suddenly, in a flash like lightning, he knew. *One on one, ten plus one*. Of course, eleven men in a cricket team.

Faster than a shot from a gun. The ball, bowled so fast that the batsman needed protection from it.

Thrice will chime the sound of a bell. Yes, it was three o'clock.

Then you'll face a bat out of hell. Not a bat as in little flying animal, but a bat as in *cricket* bat.

51

The bat out of hell hovered in front of him now, waiting for the ball. Bobcat let it fly with all his strength. Incredibly the bat caught it sideways, and it hit the wicket.

"Out!" called Sir. "Last man out!"

Bobcat looked across the field to where Dandelion still sat with Samantha, still not watching. He had to get to her, and tell her, but not when there was anyone else to hear. He stood there in the middle of the field, feeling helpless, squinting disbelievingly at the enormous number of runs on the scoreboard.

He tried to think. He mustn't get distracted by the cryptic clue. He was captain, and must think about the match. He would make changes in the batting order. He and Joe would have to go in first, instead of leaving it to Hughey Smith as he'd planned. Hughey was good, but susceptible to pressure. And if this wasn't pressure, he didn't know what was.

"Catterick!" Sir's hand landed on Bobcat's shoulder.

"Yes, sir?"

"Know what you're doing, do you?"

"Yes, I think so. Me and Joe Whittle are going in first."

"Joe Whittle and I," corrected Sir. "Good man."

After tea Bobcat put on the smelly, close-fitting helmet and the dirty pads and went in first, with Joe at the other end. The St Barnabas bowler was very fast. The ball whizzed through the air like shrapnel – unpredictable and very, very fast. Bobcat swiped, but far too late. Too late to realize that his eye wasn't in and he should have taken some practice shots during tea. Too late to pretend that the St Barnabas wicket-keeper wasn't holding up the ball in triumph, while his fellow team members danced joyfully around him.

"Out!" called Sir.

Bobcat lay face down on the grass and tried not to cry. He knew he'd cry later, when the house was dark and silent, like he heard Lizzie crying sometimes. But as captain he had to take his team's inevitable defeat in a sports-manlike way. Slowly, without looking at anyone, he got up and walked towards the bench.

"Bad luck, Catterick," said Sir, taking his hat off and wiping his forehead with it. "Can't win 'em all."

"No, sir."

"There's always next year."

Bobcat looked up at him. He couldn't see his eyes because his spectacles were reflecting the sunlight. "Next year we'll all be at the comp, sir, so I'll be in the same team as some of this lot." Bitterly he sat down and began to remove his pads. "If I even *make* the team, that is."

"Courage, boy," murmured Sir, and turned his attention to the match.

Bobcat couldn't look. He felt physically, wretchedly sick. And not just about getting caught out for a duck. About the crazy way the clue actually seemed to have something to do with real life. And about Dandelion's predictions, too.

She had told him he was a fool not to believe in her fantasy world. So was he?

She had told him he would lose the cricket match, and he had.

She had told Joe that United would lose the Cup Final.

So would they?

DANDELION AND THE DEATH OF CAESAR

It was dark in the balloon basket. Bobcat had never imagined it would be big enough for the three boys to crawl into with room to spare, when it looked so small under the vastness of the balloon itself.

"All right in there, boys?" called Ollie's dad.

It was Saturday morning, the day of the Cup Final. Joe was already wearing his United strip, and had painted his face with the team colours. Bobcat and Ollie, though dressed in ordinary clothes, were no less excited. Especially since the day had been made extra exciting by Ollie's dad's unexpected invitation.

"Why don't you all come down tomorrow morning and see the balloon take off?" he'd suggested when he'd collected Ollie from the cricket match. "We're doing some trials for the Cork run. It'll be early, mind. Pick you up at six o'clock sharp!"

Bobcat's mum hadn't been pleased. "Mar*tin*," she'd complained to his dad, who'd already said Bobcat could go. "You know I don't like Ro*bert* getting interested in ballooning. It's so dangerous."

When she used the French versions of their names it was never a good sign. The more agitated she was about something, the worse her English got. And although she was forever reminding people that hot-air ballooning had been invented in France, she hated her own family's involvement in it. A cousin she'd grown up with had ditched in a river when he was nineteen and they'd never seen him again.

"It'll be all right, Paul," Dad had assured her. "Peter Wood's a sensible guy. He won't let the boys do anything but watch."

Peter Wood was Ollie's dad. "He is *not* sensible," Mum had retorted. "Don't you know that this trial they're doing tomorrow is for a race to Cork? In Ireland? Across the sea? He's mad, and I don't want my son anywhere near him."

Dad had managed to calm her down. But she had got up at half past five when Bobcat did, and had stood on the doorstep in her dressing-gown and told Ollie's dad that the boys were only to watch. Ollie's dad had looked amused. When they'd got to the field, and the basket was lying invitingly on its side, Bobcat had followed Ollie and Joe inside, and no one had objected.

"I wish we could go up," said Ollie. "I've been up hundreds of times – well, about ten – and it's *wicked*. It's like flying."

"It *is* flying, you dipstick," said Joe, fingering the rope which tethered the basket to Ollie's dad's truck. "Everything's much bigger than you'd think, isn't it, Bobcat? Look at the size of this rope."

Bobcat looked. It was certainly a tough-looking rope. It had to be, he supposed, to avoid the disaster of the balloon taking off when it shouldn't.

Joe crawled out of the basket and sat on the grass, looking back in at Bobcat and Ollie. "I think your dad's pretty brave, going up in this thing. It looks even scarier than—"

His words were obliterated by a noise like the rushing of a hurricane. The engine which drove the fan which inflated the balloon had started up. Panicking, Bobcat got up too fast, and hit his head on one of the gas cylinders strapped to the side of the basket. "It's not going to take off now, is it?" he shouted.

But no one heard him. Ollie's dad helped him and Ollie out of the basket, which was attached to the balloon by thinner, flimsy-looking ropes. The fan was very powerful, and already the silky material spread on the ground had begun to billow. But Bobcat realized with relief that it would be ages before there was enough air in the balloon for lift-off. And anyway, the basket was still anchored firmly by the thick rope attached to the parked truck.

It might be dangerous, Bobcat decided, but it was interesting. He stood with Ollie and Joe where Ollie's dad told them to stand, watching the balloon rise up, dipping and swaying in the early morning air. When it was about half inflated Ollie's dad's co-pilot started the gas burner under the balloon. Bobcat had been to enough balloon events before to know that the flame would be huge and the roar would be deafening. But he was still thrilled.

Ollie's dad had explained that the air in the balloon had to be hot in order for the balloon to rise off the ground, because of the scientific principle that hot air always rises above colder air. Once up in the sky, the burner suspended above the basket controlled the height of the balloon – more heat to go up, less to go down.

The hot air inside the balloon dragged the basket upright, and the co-pilot climbed into it. The burner roared again. Joe clutched Bobcat's shirt as the basket began to lift off the grass. Ollie's dad scrambled over the side just in time. His weight brought the basket back down again, but not for long. As he released and dropped the anchoring rope, the basket swooped upwards very fast, dragged by the huge balloon.

"Stand back, boys!" called Ollie's dad, grinning at them over the side. "Melvin'll take you home. Enjoy the match! I'll be home for supper!"

He and the co-pilot waved, and they waved back. Melvin unclipped the rope from the truck and began to wind it up. He was wearing a T-shirt with the sleeves cut off, revealing a picture of a balloon tattooed on his arm. His job was to drive the truck to where the balloon landed, and help to pack it up.

"She's off, then!" he said cheerfully. "Enjoy that, boys?"

"You bet!" Now that his feet were on the field again, Joe was confident. "It would be fantastic to go up!"

"Well, you might get the chance," said Melvin, throwing the rope into the back of the truck. "You live in Kneshworth, don't you?"

They nodded. "Peter's been asked to do tethered balloon rides at the Kneshworth Bash in a couple of weeks," said Melvin. "A quid a go, for charity. Just for a few minutes, but it'll give the kids some fun."

"Yay!" Ollie punched the air. "We'll all go up! There's room for three boys as well as a pilot in the basket, isn't there, Melvin?"

"Course there is." He opened the cab door, chuckling. "Is there room for the three of you in here, though? Hop in, and let's get you football hooligans home."

*   *   *

That evening it seemed to stay light a long time. Though it was after half past eight, Dandelion was still playing Goldilocks and the Three Bears with Lizzie in the Wendy house. Ollie, Joe and Bobcat stayed in the sitting-room, watching Bobcat's videotape of the FA Cup Final. They'd got to the bit where the Cup was being presented to Liverpool.

Without saying anything or looking at each other, they played the presentation of the Cup again. Then, just to make sure it had really happened, Bobcat wound the tape back to Liverpool's third goal – the terrible moment when they and every other United fan knew it was all over.

"I still feel sick," said Joe, his chin on his chest. "And in two weeks' time I've got to wear Liverpool strip in public for a whole afternoon!"

Ollie shook his head solemnly. "Three–two, she said, and three–two it was. How does she do it?"

"It's just luck," said Bobcat, standing up. He pressed the eject button. "Come on, let's go outside."

Ollie got up, but Joe stayed sitting on the floor with his back against the sofa. He looked up at Bobcat and Ollie with circular eyes. "She knew we'd lose the cricket match, too, didn't she? Was that just luck?" He blinked at Bobcat accusingly. "What's going on, Catterick?"

Joe rarely called Bobcat Catterick, or a git, or anything. This business with Dandelion had obviously got to him.

"How should I know how she does it? She just does." Bobcat shrugged and put his hands in his pockets. Why were they both looking at him as if he was guilty of something? "Look, she's nuts. Everyone knows that. You've got to be nuts to go around predicting the future, haven't you?"

"Like those astronomers on telly, you mean?" asked Ollie.

"Astrologers, you mean," sighed Joe. He paused, thinking. "Maybe she's got a ... what-d'you-call-it ... a gift. In Roman times, you know, they believed some people could predict the future. Roman leaders used to consult them."

Ollie clutched his forehead dramatically. "Oh, no, not the Romans again! I can't stand it!"

"Shut up and listen," said Joe. He was very interested in the Romans. "You might learn something."

"Something like those stupid numbers, you mean?" asked Ollie.

"Roman numerals are *not* stupid—"

"Go on, Joe," interrupted Bobcat.

"Well, Caesar's death was foretold by one of these fortune-tellers, but he didn't believe it," explained Joe, getting his bright-eyed look. "He should have, though, because it came true. Just like United losing three–two. I mean, the next time Dandelion predicts something, don't you think we'd better believe her?"

They stared at him.

"Well? What do you think?"

Ollie, who preferred action to talk, suddenly lunged at Joe. He pushed Joe's shoulders down and sat astride his stomach, gripping his sides with the toes of his trainers. "I think you're as loony as her, that's what I think."

"Get off!" gasped Joe. "Just get off, will you?"

Bobcat, who was bigger than Joe and considerably bigger than Ollie, grabbed Ollie's arms and pulled him off. "*You're* the loony, Ollie."

He was annoyed enough to raise his voice. Joe looked at him, puzzled. He waited while Ollie wrestled free of Bobcat's grip, then he asked, "What's eating you?"

"Nothing."

This wasn't true. Something was eating Bobcat, but it was too shameful to admit.

The fact was, he was glad United hadn't won the Cup. If they had, Dandelion would have had to wear Joe's sister's old dandelion costume at the Bash, and carry a potty round. She would have done it, too, he had no doubt. But the prospect of Mum and Dad's fury had been keeping him awake ever since Joe had made the suggestion.

He looked out of the window. Dandelion was lumbering across the lawn, chasing a shrieking Goldilocks. That was another thing which was eating him. Lizzie liked playing with Dandelion better than she'd ever liked playing with her own brother. On top of that, and quite apart from the lucky predictions, there was the spider in the computer, and the mysterious clue, and the embarrassing tale of Harmon Major and All Its Dominions.

"Are you in a mood, Catterick?" asked Ollie.

"No, but I will be if you don't shut up about it."

"Dandelion! Lizzie!"

Mum crossed the lawn. She took hold of Lizzie's hand and steered her towards the house. Dandelion followed, still growling, with Lizzie giggling. As they passed the open window Mum called to Bobcat. "Your friends are going home *now*, Robert!"

The three boys got as far as the street, where they lingered, leaning on the garden fence.

"She's psychic, that Dandelion," said Joe.

"Whose sidekick?" asked Ollie.

"Oh, shut up," said Bobcat and Joe together.

"We've got that mural thing next week," said Joe. "Some sort of presentation."

"Sounds boring," said Ollie.

"Yep." Bobcat straightened up. He really wanted them to go. He was weary of them and everything else. "But there's indoor sports to look forward to. That's always a laugh."

"You're only saying that because you always win," said Joe.

"No I don't," said Bobcat modestly. He was good at most sports, and could climb a rope faster than any boy in the school. "I'm never any use in the tug-of-war."

"But you're bound to win the rope race," Ollie assured him. "It's your blue ribbon event."

"Blue riband, I think you mean," said Joe.

Ollie paused. "That's a chocolate biscuit, isn't it?"

"Look…" Bobcat's patience was weakening. "Just go home, will you?"

"Yeah," agreed Joe. He yawned. "I need some sleep even if Ollie doesn't."

They ambled off. Bobcat watched them for a minute, wondering how a day which started so brilliantly could end so badly. Then he went upstairs and sat on his bed. The window framed a square of purple sky. He didn't put the light on. He was so tired, he felt like going to bed with all his clothes on. But Mum wouldn't be impressed, and it was too hot anyway.

He was just beginning to take off his shirt

when Dandelion came in.

"Don't you ever knock?" Bobcat pulled his shirt down again. "And the sign on the door says—"

"I know what the sign on the door says, and I think it's very rude. Where's that clue?" She went to his desk and seized the print-out. "Is this it?" Her eyes looked strange in the bluish half-darkness of the unlit bedroom. "Listen, Bobcat, I've realized what the bat is!"

"So have I."

She was surprised. "Have you? What is it, then?"

"No, you go first." If she wanted to make a fool of herself, he might as well let her.

"Could it be a cricket bat?"

Bobcat lay down on his bed and closed his eyes. His limbs felt feeble. "It could be, I suppose."

"Is that what you thought?"

"Yes, but you don't have to believe me."

"I *do* believe you. Did you think of anything else?"

"The church clock struck three just before that horrible batsman came out," said Bobcat. "And there are eleven men in a cricket team, and the ball goes faster than a bullet. Well, maybe not faster than—"

"Oh, of course, it's the cricket match! Aren't you clever!"

"You thought of it too," he said, without

opening his eyes.

"I only thought of the bat part. I didn't even watch the match. I was talking to Samantha. I didn't know about the horrible batsman. I didn't even know there are eleven in the team. Oh, isn't this wonderful?"

Bobcat didn't think it was wonderful. He opened his eyes and propped himself up on one elbow. "Look, Dandelion. Let me get this straight. According to you, in order for you to get back to Harmon Major or whatever it's called, and rescue your mother, you've got to solve the clue. Well, now you've solved it. But a cricket match doesn't have anything to do with rescuing princesses. So where does it lead?"

She began to walk about in the small space between the bed and the desk, one hand embedded in her hair. With the other hand she flapped the print-out against her thigh. She looked pretty funny. "It leads to the next clue, of course."

"How, though?"

"By means of a password!" She stopped pacing and looked at him. The light had faded further. He could hardly see her face. "All these passwords are to do with *you*, Bobcat. *You're* the king of the Sixers, and the first password was King. It was your cricket match, so the password must be Cricket, or something to do with it. The next password will be something to do with you as well. Each clue leads to another, and when we solve the last one everything will be clear. My mother will come back to me, Bobcat, you'll see."

She sat down heavily in the chair by the desk, her head on her hand.

Bobcat's bad temper came back, stronger than before. "Why don't you stop this stupid princess nonsense?" he asked her rudely. "Everyone at school thinks you're a total freak."

She raised her head. Her face was in complete darkness now. He wondered if she'd started to cry. He saw her arm silhouetted against the window as she wiped her nose on the back of her hand. "If it's nonsense, why was the clue about something that really happened?" Her voice trembled a little.

"Coincidence," he told her confidently. He'd been amazed at first, but he'd had a day to calm down and think about it. And Ollie's remark about television astrologers had set off an idea too. "The clues must be written so that you can fit your own circumstances to them. Just like horoscopes."

Suddenly she snapped on the desk light. Bobcat blinked. "Hey, I didn't ask you to—"

"Let's go down to Dad's study and call up Tarantula again! You type in Cricket and let's see what happens." When he didn't move she got impatient. "Come on, Bobcat, it's important!"

"I'm not allowed to use the computer without Dad's permission," he told her. He sat up and put his feet on the floor, though.

"Then get his permission! Move, will you?" Bobcat moved.

Dad didn't understand what was so urgent, but Dandelion promised they'd only be a few minutes.

"Have you been crying, Dandelion?" he asked. "What's wrong?"

"Nothing. I'm fine, honest."

Dad shrugged at Bobcat and went back to his TV programme. "I want you both ready for bed in twenty minutes!" he called from the hall.

Bobcat was quicker this time. The keys chattered, and Tarantula appeared.

"Type in Cricket," said Dandelion.

Bobcat did so, and pressed ENTER. As before, the screen flashed with silver light, which faded to reveal a rhyme. It was the second clue.

I creep to the sky, I follow the hours,
Turning my face to the passing
    of time.
Bewitched by my beauty?
    Then come with me,
For the spell will lead you to clue
    number three.

Bobcat's heart sank. "Witches and spells and

fairy tales," he said scornfully. "*You* can deal with this one, Dandelion. Just leave me out of it."

BOBCAT AND THE DOUBLE DISASTER

"Catterick! What the *hell's* the matter with you?"

This was serious. Sir never said hell, or damn, or even blessed or bloomin', like other teachers. Bobcat went very hot and very cold again. "Don't know, sir."

Sir's face was pink with frustration. His narrow lips were narrower than usual. He polished his glasses on the hem of his sports shirt. The afternoon sun, streaming through the windows of the school hall, shone on his small, sad eyes.

"I can't help it, sir," blurted out Bobcat. "I know I can climb fast, but I just can't do it today."

They'd been doing indoor sports trials for two days now. Bobcat hadn't performed very well yesterday in any of the sprint races, or the individual rope-climbing, but Sir had muttered

70

about an "off day" and put his name at the top of the list as usual. Today, though, Sir was selecting boys for the rope-climbing relay, the final and, in Ollie's words, "blue ribbon" event.

It was awful. Bobcat knew, and Sir knew, and so did everyone else, that he didn't deserve his place. Other boys had climbed better in their trials, and should be given the chance. Yet Sir understood how important Bobcat's very last Kneshworth indoor sports day was, and how desperately he wanted to be on the team.

Poor old Sir. He wanted to be fair, but he didn't want to dump his star. It was making him say hell, and it was all because of Dandelion.

Bobcat stood there, feeling conspicuous. "Confess, Catterick," said Sir, not sharply, but not kindly either. "Has someone put lead in your shoes? Or cold Yorkshire pudding, perhaps?"

Girls giggled and boys snorted. Bobcat didn't say anything. He could hear Dandelion's high-pitched trill over the top of all the other sounds. It's your fault, Dandelion Primrose Compost-Heap Slug-Pellet Gardener, he told her silently. It's all your stupid fantasy-believing, result-predicting, Lizzie-spoiling fault.

Dandelion had taken away his confidence in

himself. If she hadn't correctly predicted the result of the cricket match, and if United hadn't lost the Cup Final so spectacularly, and if Joe hadn't been so miserable about having to wear Liverpool strip, and gone on so stupidly about Caesar not believing the fortune-teller, he'd have run and climbed perfectly well. But without the will to win, as Sir always said, you'd certainly lose.

Sir looked at him carefully, then at his wrist-watch. He blew his whistle. "Go and get changed, then, you lot. The list will be up in the classroom tomorrow. And Bobcat ... I mean, Catterick..."

"Yes, sir?"

"If you're not on it, you'll know why, won't you?"

Bobcat nodded miserably. "Yes, sir."

"Run along, then."

He really did have to run, or he'd be late meeting Lizzie at the Infants' gate. He charged off. But at the corner of the building something slammed into him, almost knocking him over. It was Samantha Pilkington. She wasn't hurt, but she was angry.

"You clumsy idiot!" she shouted crossly. "You should have tried running as fast as that in the sprint trials!"

Bobcat wanted to tell her to shut up, or worse, but he hadn't the breath. His insides felt wobbly and hollow, like a hot-water bottle before you put the water in.

Samantha wasn't used to being ignored. "Aren't you going to apologize?"

"What for? It was an accident," he panted. "You might as well apologize to me."

She gave him such an evil look that for a moment he thought she was going to spit at him. "You wait, Catterick!" Her voice sounded thick, as if she had a cold. "I'll get you!"

She walked off, swinging her schoolbag.

"In your dreams, Pilkington!" called Bobcat.

After all his hurry, Lizzie wasn't even out when he got to the Infants' School. The sound of singing floated from the open windows. He stood a little way away from the groups of chatting mothers, trying not to think about indoor sports day or Samantha Pilkington. Instead, he thought about the second clue.

I creep to the sky, I follow the hours,
Turning my face to the passing
    of time.
Bewitched by my beauty?
    Then come with me,
For the spell will lead you to clue
    number three.

Although he'd refused to help Dandelion solve it, he'd learnt it by heart. He couldn't stop himself, somehow. The Tarantula game was a good, clever idea. Solving clues was fun. Why hadn't Joe, who knew more about computers than all the other boys in the class, ever told him and Ollie about it? And why had Dad installed it in the computer at home, and not let on? Knowing Dad, he played it himself when Bobcat was in bed. All dads were big kids, he thought, like Ollie's dad with his balloon.

Whose face was it, in the clue? And if it wasn't a person, what else had a face? Dandelion had suggested each clue might have something to do with Bobcat himself. He looked at his watch. A watch had a face, and hours, and showed the passing of time. And the first clue had had something about time in it, too.

A watch didn't creep to the sky, though. What did? If the clue was about his own life, what did he do which involved creeping to the sky?

Rope-climbing? His heart bulged. He frowned, thinking hard. The ropes only went to the ceiling, but – his heart bulged again – the *balloon* went to the sky.

No, that couldn't be it. There was no chance that he could ever go up in a balloon. The clue was a bit too fairyland-ish for him. He decided to see if he could get into Tarantula without Dandelion, and find different clues with different passwords. Monsters or warriors, or even cartoon characters, would be better than Dandelion's girlish version of the game.

He turned his attention to the children spilling from the gate. "Hey, Liz!" he called.

She headed for him, skipping, and thrust a note into his hand. "Mule tomorrow!"

"What?" He looked at the note. It was a reminder that the presentation of the certificate for the playground mural was taking place tomorrow at half past two. He stuffed it in his bag. "Oh, the mural. The fuss they're making, anyone would think it's important."

"It is 'portant. It's going in the newspaper, Miss Preston says." Lizzie skipped along beside him. "Why can't we have a mule in *our* playground?"

"It's a *mural*, not a mule, Liz. You know what a mural is, don't you?"

"Course. It's an aminal. Like a donkey. I hope it kicks Miss Preston. She's horrible."

Bobcat was laughing almost too much to speak. "When are you going to get a–ni–mal the right way round?" he asked her. "And a mural isn't an animal anyway – it's a painting on a wall."

"Is that all?" Lizzie stopped skipping. Her nose wrinkled in disappointment.

He nodded gravely. "That's all. It's not going to kick anyone. A mural isn't even alive."

They walked on in the sunshine. And it

wasn't until ages afterwards that Bobcat remembered what he said that day, and wondered if *he* was the one with the gift for predicting the future.

Mr Alfred Winstanley, the leader of Spenmouth Council, was an anxious-looking man who kept swallowing, as if he had a cough sweet permanently in his mouth. His eyes darted around the crowd of parents, mural painters, Kneshworth children and the man from the *Advertiser*, who had gathered to watch the presentation of the certificate. When Mrs Goodman introduced him, he swallowed more rapidly, and blinked too.

"Most honoured, Mrs Goodman," he said, putting his mouth so close to the microphone that it popped. His amplified voice echoed against the playground walls. He jumped. "I'll have to get used to this," he added.

Maybe he's only just been elected, thought Bobcat.

Mrs Goodman took his place at the microphone, smiling. She *never* smiled when parents weren't there. After seven years at Kneshworth, Bobcat knew that for a fact.

"Welcome, everybody," she said brightly. "As you all know, we are here this afternoon to accept an award from Spenmouth Council for our contribution to local environmental improvement."

There was a pause while she considered how to explain this official-sounding phrase. "Making our surroundings more fun to play in," she said. Then she went back to her notes. "As you see, the mural is almost finished. In fact, we have our trusty team of painters ready to put the final touches to it as we speak!"

The mural had been painted by three teenage girls from Spenmouth Comprehensive School on an art project. They hovered in front of it, wearing overalls and smiling shyly. It was of a jungle scene, with lions. Joe had pointed out that lions don't live in jungles, but no one had taken any notice.

"These young ladies have, of course, been aided and abetted by Kneshworth children, who have put in a lot of work, especially near the bottom of the painting!"

There was some laughter and clapping from the parents. Bobcat was glad that Mum was teaching her French conversation class, and that Dad, who was a landscape gardener, had gone to Birmingham to see someone's garden.

"Now, I call upon Mr Winstanley to declare the final painting session under way, and when the last brush stroke has been made, let's have a nice big round of applause as the children receive the certificate on behalf of the school. Mr Photographer, stand by!"

Mrs Goodman withdrew, and the leader of

the council stepped up to the microphone again. "Off you go, then, girls!" he said self-consciously.

Off they went. One climbed the stepladder and began to shade the undersides of some palm leaves. Another had left the tuft off a lion's tail deliberately so that she could paint it in now. The other girl, a young-looking one with a ponytail, who reminded Bobcat of Lizzie, turned her attention to the sunflowers painted in the corner where the mural spread to the next wall.

But before she'd managed to get her brush out of the paint pot, she leapt backwards, so quickly that she fell over, upsetting the paint all over the neatly swept tarmac. "Oh my God, look! *Look!*" She scrambled to her feet, pointing hysterically at the corner of the mural. "It *moved*!" she exclaimed. "That plant – it's *alive*!"

Bobcat craned his neck to see. Incredibly, the plant *was* moving. Slinky, bright green stems writhed like worms round the corner. The petals of the sunflower – which, Bobcat noticed, was much smaller than all the others – nodded slowly from side to side, with real eyes in its round face.

His horror subsided. It wasn't a plant at all. But relief soon changed to astonishment, and astonishment back to horror of a different kind. "Oh, no!" he wailed, not caring who heard him.

Emerging from the corner, wearing nothing but a green swimming costume, and with every inch of her body covered in green paint, was Dandelion. She was grinning so widely that her teeth made an eerie white slash across her green face. At the top of the green stalk she'd made of herself, she had gelled the dandelion fronds of her hair into a halo of petals, invisible at first among the other explosions of yellow on the wall behind her. She spread her green arms. "Hello, everyone! Look, I'm in the mural! A dandelion in the jungle!"

The man from the *Advertiser* couldn't believe his luck. Mrs Goodman, her eyes popping, didn't have time, it turned out, to get out of the picture he took of Dandelion. Gleefully he photographed the indignation on the faces of the teenage girls, whose big moment had been so cruelly stolen from them. His camera click-clicked away at the hysterical parents and shrieking children.

He thrust a tape-recorder under Dandelion's nose and asked her questions about herself. He scribbled in his notebook as she spelled out her surname, and told him her mother was a princess imprisoned in a distant country. And all the time he smirked. What had promised to be a report interesting only to those whose names were mentioned in it had turned into a front-page scoop.

Suddenly Bobcat lost his temper. Two disasters in two days was too much for him to stand. The grievances that he'd tried to keep under control broke free. Rage like he'd never known rushed through his body.

"Dandelion!" he shouted through the laughter and applause. "You psycho, you'll regret this!"

She must have had help with the green paint and the hair gel. He looked wildly around the playground. Samantha Pilkington was leaning against one of the unpainted walls, laughing. Bobcat's anger grew. This pathetic partnership Dandelion had formed with Samantha Pilkington was the final kick in his face.

Without knowing what he was going to do, he strode towards her. His voice came out like a squeak. "You're in trouble, Pilkington!"

"In your dreams, Catterick!" She stopped laughing, though.

Dandelion appeared. She gave Bobcat a puzzled look. "What's the matter? Didn't you like my joke?"

Bobcat wasn't in control of himself. He grabbed Dandelion and pushed her, hard, against the wall. "You snotty little toad! You're completely bonkers, aren't you? Just because you haven't got any parents, you think it's all right to act like a nutcase and tell fairy tales so that everyone will feel sorry for you. Don't you?"

Dandelion stood there, her eyes and mouth widening. But now he'd started, he couldn't stop. "I bet your mother abandoned you, and I don't blame her!" he shouted.

Dandelion didn't cry. She seemed to have been turned to stone. But Samantha hadn't. And, he noticed too late, neither had a girl called Verity Simmonds who used to hang around with Samantha before Dandelion came. Against them both, he didn't have a chance.

"You pig!" screamed Samantha, and hit him with her schoolbag. There was something heavy inside it which crashed down on Bobcat's upper arm, making him cry out.

"Come on, Verity, kick him!" called Samantha.

Verity didn't need to be asked twice. Before Bobcat could move Verity had inflicted a kick worse than any football foul on the back of his knee. His leg jackknifed, and he fell heavily against the wall.

Then, in the space of a few seconds, several things happened. Bobcat couldn't remember, when he thought about it afterwards, which came first. He heard Joe's voice above the girls' screeching, and Samantha fell over on her bottom in a very unladylike way. It should have been funny, but Bobcat was too furious

81

to care. Dandelion's orange hair and green face seemed suddenly very close. He felt something squashy, which could have been a body or a bag, and heard someone's jerky, uneven breathing. His own, probably. He was crammed in the angle between the wall and the playground. It hurt to move, so he didn't bother.

Then a strong hand grasped the back of his shirt collar and hauled him to his feet. It was Mrs Goodman.

Samantha, Verity and Joe – if he'd ever been there – had disappeared. There was only Dandelion leaning against the wall, still not crying, still staring at him with her weird eyes in her weird green face.

Mrs Goodman dragged him and Dandelion towards the school building. "If you want to be in that rope race, Robert Catterick," she said, her stubby fingers digging into his neck, "you'd better have a good explanation for this behaviour!"

"It's her, not me!" Bobcat almost screamed.

"That's *enough*!"

It was fruitless. He might as well scream at the mural. Hot, and almost in tears, and unable to believe that Dandelion had reduced him to this state of girlish wretchedness, he stumbled into Mrs Goodman's office. Dandelion tried to run away, but Mrs Goodman caught her by the strap of her swimsuit. Just before the door shut he heard the microphone pop again, and Mr Winstanley's bewildered voice floated across the playground.

"Er … shall I present the certificate now?"

DANDELION AND THE FIENDISH ROPE TRICK

Sir slammed the *Children's Encyclopedia of Plants and Animals* onto his desk. There was silence. Even Dandelion and Samantha stopped babbling. Nineteen pairs of eyes followed Sir as he replaced the book and brushed chalk dust from the front of his jumper.

"A serious task…" He folded his arms, looking ponderously around at each face. "A *very* serious task has to be completed today. Are you all ready?"

"Yes, sir," they droned obediently.

Bobcat wondered uneasily what could be coming next.

"Samantha Pilkington, Verity Simmonds and Dandelion Gardener, stand up."

Bobcat's heart leapt into his throat. Sir knew about the fight, then. As Dandelion rose to her feet with the other girls, she turned and looked at him. A fine brother you are, her eyes said. This is *your* problem, not mine.

"What about me, sir?" asked Joe bravely. "I was there too. And don't you want Robert Catterick, too?"

While Joe had been speaking, Sir's expression had changed from sternness to bewilderment, then to amusement. "Well, Joseph Whittle," he said to Joe. "You and Catterick really are a comedy double act, aren't you?"

Joe didn't risk saying anything.

"I mean…" Sir's control over his face was weakening. "If you two would like to stand up too, we'd be happy to consider both of you for the title of carnival princess. Wouldn't we, Year Six?"

Bobcat hoped his face hadn't gone as red as Joe's. The laughter was embarrassing, but easier to bear than the public disgrace he'd feared. He laughed, but Joe's face remained unmoved. Joe really hated looking foolish in front of Sir.

"That'll teach you to jump to conclusions, Whittle," said Sir, still chuckling. "Maybe next year, eh? Carnival prince?"

The three girls were still standing up. Samantha was simpering. Dandelion had flushed beetroot with self-importance. Only thin, fair-haired Verity had the grace to show any astonishment.

"*Me*, sir?" she exclaimed. "But Samantha said—"

"Never mind what Samantha said," Sir told her briskly. "You three girls have been nominated by the organizing committee of the Kneshworth Bash and Ball to be considered for the title this year." He gave the class a how-did-I-get-myself-into-this look, though Bobcat could tell he was enjoying himself. "And it's your privilege as top of the school, Year Six, to decide which girl is to be the princess and which her handmaidens. Better than doing maths, isn't it?"

Ollie had sat still longer than he could bear. He jumped up, almost knocking over his chair. "Please, sir, can I collect the votes? Are those yellow things the voting slips? Can I give them out?"

Sir let him and Hughey Smith give out and collect the carefully folded slips. Bobcat listened to the cheerful chatter around him, wondering what they were all so excited about. Everyone knew what the outcome of the voting would be.

There wasn't a girl or a boy in the whole class brave enough to vote for anyone but Samantha.

He thought about it. Girls who crossed Samantha could expect to lose all their friends before lunchtime. And she treated boys like servants, or halfwits. One day Bobcat had come back to his table to find that a pink flower-border had appeared round the neat copy of his English homework. "But I thought you'd like it!" Samantha had protested, pouting. "I was *sure* a clever boy like you would have the same taste as me!"

Dandelion had suffered, too, despite her so-called friendship with Samantha. When she'd come back from PE to find someone had upset nail varnish all over her skirt, Samantha hadn't sympathized. Bobcat had heard her exclaim, "Goodness, Dandelion, how original you are! I've got some exactly like that, but silly me – I wear it on my nails!" He'd wondered if she was the one who'd spilt it. On purpose.

Bobcat bit the end of his already bite-marked pencil. The vote was secret, after all. No one would recognize his printing even if they saw his paper. He didn't want to vote for Samantha, but he couldn't bring himself to vote for Dandelion either. Before he could change his mind he wrote down *Verity Simmonds*, folded the yellow paper up very small and tossed it into Hughey Smith's shoebox.

It was useless, and almost as cowardly as voting for Samantha would have been. But it gave him satisfaction to do it. He waited expectantly while Sir tipped the votes out onto his desk and made sure all sixteen people eligible to vote had done so.

"In the event of a tie between two contestants, I have the casting vote. And there'll be no arguments." He unfolded the first paper, and put it down on the corner of the desk.

The next vote went on the same pile, and the next. Bobcat's insides settled.

The whole thing was going to be boringly predictable. And the carnival parade was boring anyway. Why should it matter to him who won the vote?

"Oh good, someone different," said Sir.

Bobcat sat up. The piece of paper Sir had just unfolded wasn't the one he'd written Verity's name on. He'd folded his into distinctive triangles, so he could tell.

Someone else had voted for Verity, or perhaps even for Dandelion.

Bobcat looked at Dandelion, wondering what she was thinking. She was sitting with her elbows on the table and her fists pressed into her cheeks. The light from the open window made her hair and face as bright as gold. She looked very happy. Bobcat's insides jumped as he remembered Joe's words about Caesar's death. She knew what was going to happen.

"*And* someone else," announced Sir, and started a third pile of papers. The next one he picked up was Bobcat's. He put it on the second pile. The next one was for Verity too, and the three after that went on the third pile. Were they for Samantha? Or could they actually be for *Dandelion*?

Gradually a silence descended on the

classroom. No one looked at anyone else, in case their faces betrayed their treason. Joe kept twitching his glasses up. Someone was tapping their foot against the leg of their chair.

The piles of paper grew. Like everyone else in the room, Bobcat couldn't stop himself looking at Samantha. But for the first time in her life she seemed unwilling to be looked at. She sat with her hands clasped on the desk in front of her, staring at nothing.

"Right," said Sir, putting the last paper on its pile. "Oliver Wood, would you be my checker?"

Sir counted. Then Ollie counted and Sir wrote the numbers down. When Ollie had returned to his seat, Sir stood up. He didn't seem to be enjoying himself any more. "Samantha Pilkington, five votes," he said.

Silence.

"Verity Simmonds, five votes."

Silence, while everyone did the same sum in their heads.

"Dandelion Gardener, six votes." He looked at Dandelion, who was still sitting by the window, her chin on her fists. "Congratulations, Dandelion. You've been chosen as this year's carnival princess."

No one spoke, or hugged Dandelion, or anything. They sat there like rag dolls. Then Samantha slammed the palms of her hands on the table and stood up.

"But it *can't* be her!" Her eyes looked watery, but no tears fell. "She's so ugly, she'll look *terrible* in that lovely dress! It'll spoil the parade for everyone, and … and it's just not *fair*!"

Sir's expression didn't change. "The vote *was* fair, Samantha, so you've just got to accept it."

"I *won't*!"

"I won't *sir*," Sir reminded her. "And you'll be telling Mrs Goodman about it, if you don't watch out."

"Can't we do it again?" she pleaded.

"Certainly not." Sir gathered up the voting papers. "We've wasted enough time this morning already. Dandelion, your parents will receive a letter from the organizing committee. Now, let's get on with some maths."

Samantha tried some sobbing, but Sir told her to be quiet and not get tears on her maths book. No one else took any notice. Even the two girls apart from Verity who were in her gang, and who must have been among the five who voted for her, could only give her sympathetic looks.

Silently, stealthily, a feeling of achievement crept over the classroom. A feeling of joy, almost. Bobcat suspected that the crowd at the carnival parade would be bigger than usual. People would turn up to enjoy the spectacle of Samantha Pilkington *not* being the carnival princess.

And, of course, to gawp at Dandelion.

Everyone had seen, or heard about, the mural incident. Everyone had heard Dandelion's story about her mother being crown princess of a distant country. Everyone had heard her say that one day she – *she* – would be Dandelion Primrose, Crown Princess of Harmon Major and All Its Dominions. What would she make of this very public opportunity to be a princess already?

Bobcat tied the laces of his trainers, wondering why his fingers felt frozen on such a warm afternoon. There was no one else left in the classroom. Thinking about what was about to happen made his stomach feel as if he'd eaten a huge helping of sponge pudding and custard.

Indoor sports day was his one chance to show that he was still King of the Sixers. He could do it, too, if he could only get his confidence back from wherever Dandelion had thrown it.

He couldn't stop thinking about Tarantula's second clue. *Bewitched by my beauty?* Well, that *couldn't* be anything to do with Dandelion. Samantha was the prettiest girl in the class by miles. Could the clue be something to do with her? Could Samantha be the next password? If so, what did all that stuff about the passing of time mean? He wished it would go away and stop disturbing his concentration.

Dandelion's predictions were disturbing him too. Could she really be some kind of mystic, with a gift for seeing the future? If so, should he actually *ask* her what was going to happen today? But if he did that, how could he even *enter* the rope race, knowing his strength and agility had nothing to do with the outcome – win or lose?

"Come on, Bobcat, leg it!" called Joe from the hall.

Bobcat joined him and the other Greens. Ollie, who was in Blue House, catcalled to them. "We're going to beat you, you pack of losers!"

Bobcat and Joe looked at each other. "They *are* going to beat us, aren't they?" said Bobcat. "Or Red House are."

"Why?" asked Joe calmly. "We've got loads of good kids in Green. We're favourites for the tug-of-war. And you go up that rope like a monkey."

"I don't know," shrugged Bobcat. By Jupiter, he felt depressed. "I've just got a funny feeling about it."

Joe rolled his eyes. "A funny feeling? That's for girls! You sound like that daft sister of yours."

"She's not my sister, she's—"

"Yeah, yeah, we know. Look, calm down

and think about pulping the opposition – that's what we're here for."

"But what can I do about it?"

"What?"

"The funny feeling. How can I win, if Dandelion's willing me to lose?"

"Who says she's willing you to lose?"

"I don't know. I can't explain." Bobcat began to feel as foolish as Joe thought he was. "It's just a feeling. It's like she's watching me. It's like she's controlling me."

Joe frowned. "Those spooky predictions, you mean?"

"Not just those. It's the way she's taken over everything. Nothing's the same any more."

"Look, Bobcat," said Joe patiently. "I know I said that the next time Dandelion predicts something we'd better believe her – and I still think that. But what has she said about this afternoon?"

Bobcat shrugged unhappily.

"Exactly," said Joe. "Zero, zilch, nada. The only thing she can think about is dressing up as this stupid princess on Saturday. Princess Dandelion, I ask you!"

"Did I hear my name, Joe Whittle?"

Dandelion was hanging from the wall bars. The draught from the open doors blew ragged strands of hair over her face. She was wearing a red sash across her chest.

"Hello, Bobcat!" she cried. "I'm in the

three-legged race with Verity! Now, what did I come over for? Oh, I know! To wish you luck in the rope-climbing. Sorry you're not in the relay, but everyone wants you to win the individual, even us lot in Red House!"

Bobcat and Joe stared at her.

"Everyone says you're so good!" she added, her eyes bright. "I *know* you'll win. I just know it!"

She dropped to the floor and ran off to join the Reds, her gangly arms and legs flying. Joe kicked Bobcat's ankle gently with the toe of his trainer.

"See? She loves you! And now she's predicted it, we've got to believe it, haven't we? Go on, they're calling the first sprint heat."

Bobcat got up and jogged to the starting line. He heard Joe, who would be in the second heat, shouting behind him. "Go, Catterick! Go, Greens!"

Bobcat won his heat.

During the sprint final, he could hear Dandelion's voice above everyone else's. When he dashed over the line three strides ahead of the others, and crashed, sweating, into the padded end wall of the hall, he realized why. Looking up, he saw that she'd climbed the wall bars and was sitting on the very top one like a tropical bird.

"That's my brother!" she was screeching, louder than any parrot. "Look, everyone!

That's my *brother*!"

Red House won the tug-of-war, but Dandelion and Verity fell over, red-faced, in the three-legged race. Verity didn't laugh, though. She was the kind of girl who didn't do things for a laugh.

He thought about how horrible she and Samantha had been to him during the fight he'd had with Dandelion. Why? It wasn't even their fight. And they hadn't been defending Dandelion from him – he'd barely touched her. It was Joe who'd had to defend *him* from *them* in the end.

Like everything else, it was all because of Dandelion. How pointless it had been to worry about her having to wear a dandelion costume at the Bash! She'd made her own dandelion costume anyway, and appeared in it on the front page of the *Advertiser*. A DANDELION AMONG THE SUNFLOWERS, the headline had read.

Sunflowers.

Names were being called for the first heat of the rope-climbing race, but Bobcat didn't listen. Sunflowers. Famous for growing very tall, and turning their faces to the sun as it travelled across the sky. Wasn't that why they were called sunflowers? Or was it because their bright yellow petals made them look like children's drawings of the sun? It had to be something to do with the mural.

Dandelion was at his side, looking worried. "Come on, Bobcat, it's your heat!"

"It's got to be something to do with the mural," he told her.

"What? Come *on*, get to your rope or they'll start without you."

She pushed him forwards. He almost fell over, but managed to grasp the bottom of the rope before Sir blew the starting whistle. He shinned to the top of the rope and pressed the buzzer. Hughey Smith beat him, but he didn't care – it was only a heat, and three boys went through to the final.

He slid down, not too fast. He wasn't wearing gloves. Dandelion hadn't gone back to the Reds. She was waiting at the bottom of the rope, her eyes wide. "What did you say about the mural?"

"Second heat!" called Sir. Six more boys rushed to the ropes. Bobcat pulled Dandelion out of their way.

"It's the sunflowers. The thing in the clue which turns its face to the passing of time is a *sunflower*."

"I thought you weren't going to help me with this clue. I thought you said—"

"Well, anyway. Don't you think the next password could be Sunflower?"

She sat down on a bench. "Maybe. But what's the bit about the spell?"

"I don't know." Bobcat sat down too. The

muscles in his legs felt wobbly. "What does a spell do?"

"Magicks things," suggested Dandelion. "Makes them appear or disappear."

This didn't seem to mean much. They both thought hard. "What else?" asked Bobcat.

"Oh, I know!" She clapped her hands in excitement. "Spells make things come alive! You know, like in *Pinocchio*."

Bobcat stared at her. "And the girl thought…"

"The mural was coming alive! Wasn't it funny? It certainly livened up that dreary presentation!" Her face clouded a little. "It wasn't a spell, though. I mean, I'm not a witch, am I?"

Sir was calling the names for the rope-climbing final. Bobcat stood up and walked self-consciously to the bottom of his rope. Green House cheered. He looked up. The buzzer button looked very far away.

Hughey Smith was next to him, spitting on his hands. Joe was in the final too, with Matt Henson, a boy of about Bobcat's size who had recently joined the school, and hadn't taken part in last year's indoor sports. The other two were outsiders with no chance.

"Right, boys." Sir walked to the centre of the hall, his whistle at the ready. Everyone was quiet. "Usual rules. When I blow this whistle, off you go. First to buzz is the winner, second to buzz is second, and so on. Last two drop out, then four go up again. Last two drop out and the two remaining boys go up. Ready?"

Bobcat was as ready as he'd ever be. He grabbed the rope and climbed as fast as he could. His legs felt heavy – it must be nerves – but when the buzzer was in reach he stretched and, to his relief, it sounded first. The other buzzes were almost drowned by the cheering.

In the second round it was his arms which felt wrong. His hands were sweaty and didn't seem to be gripping the rope properly. As he neared the top the buzzer seemed to be getting further and further away. His arm wasn't long enough.

"First, Robert Catterick!" declared Sir.

Bobcat slid down. He wiped his hands on his T-shirt, wondering how he'd managed to sound the buzzer first. His body felt as wooden as Pinocchio's before the fairy put the spell on him.

Don't think about spells. Climb the rope.

It was him against the untested Matt Henson. Bobcat looked warily at Matt's sturdy limbs. Butterflies flapped in his stomach. Matt, who was in Red House, was going to get to the buzzer first. Green House's hopes of victory, which Bobcat had carried on his shoulders since he'd won the sprint final half an hour ago, would be dashed. He would be in disgrace because of Dandelion.

Again.

His exasperation was stronger than his arms or legs. He grasped the rope. Maybe if he pretended the rope was Dandelion's scrawny little arms, which he could twist until she screamed, he'd get to the top first. Looking up, he saw her perched on the top wall bar, hanging on with one hand and waving at him with the other. "Go, Bobcat!" she yelled. "You're going to win!"

So that was her final prediction, was it? Bobcat's palms felt sore against the rope. He wished the race were over. Silence fell, and the whistle blew.

Up, up for the third time he went. He felt as if he'd been doing this for ever. Surely last year's final hadn't been so exhausting? Or had he just been having more fun that day? Somehow this didn't seem fun any more. It seemed like hard, hard work. Cheering filled his ears. "Matt! Matt! Matt!" Was anyone chanting his own name? Dandelion's squawk had disappeared under the tidal wave of noise.

Somehow, he got to the top. But when he reached out for the buzzer, the muscles in the arm which was still holding the rope weakened suddenly. The whole school gasped. He grabbed the rope with his buzzer-hand and clung there, swaying dizzily. He wasn't sure if he'd pressed the buzzer or not. But if he hadn't, Matt Henson certainly had.

The cheering had stopped. Bobcat heard

Dandelion's horrified voice, quite nearby, call, "Bobcat, don't fall!"

Sir caught the end of the swinging rope, planting his feet firmly and spreading his free arm to balance himself. The face he turned up to Bobcat was full of alarm. "Hang on!" he called. "Try to come down slowly. Don't slide, you'll burn your hands."

Bobcat looked down. The floor looked much further away than usual. Sir's white face loomed in front of it. Matt Henson had slid down his rope and was looking up at Bobcat too. Mrs Goodman's arm was round his shoulders.

"Come on, you lot!" ordered Sir. "Pile up as many mats as you can find under this rope!"

They scampered to do it, and Sir turned back to Bobcat. "You've won!" he called. "Your buzzer sounded first. Get down safely and we'll present the trophy. Green House have won!"

Bobcat's arms ached. He couldn't feel the rope curling against his bare legs, though he knew it must be there. Dandelion, high up on the wall bars, was almost as far off the ground as he was.

"We've done it, Bobcat!" she told him.

We've done it?

There was no strength left in Bobcat's limbs. He couldn't hold on any more. "Help!" he croaked, and let go.

The mats helped, but he fell mainly on top of Sir. Sir's glasses fell off and Bobcat's weight smashed them. He lay there, with Mrs Goodman fussing and Sir grunting. "Sorry," he said shakily. "Sorry about your glasses, sir." Then, after a pause, "Did I really hit the buzzer first?"

It seemed he had, and Green House won the trophy. When they'd hoisted it and had their photograph taken, Bobcat felt better. He sat down on the bench and thought. In his heart, he knew he hadn't pressed the buzzer. But it had sounded. So if he hadn't pressed it, who had? No one else had been near enough. Even Dandelion. He took Dandelion's arm and eased her into the deserted corridor.

"Come on, tell me how you did it."

Mischief came into her eyes. "Promise not to tell Mum?"

"*Mum?*" Surely it was Sir, or Mrs Goodman, he shouldn't be telling?

"Well…" She looked up and down the corridor, then pulled up the hem of her T-shirt. There, attached to the waistband of her shorts, was the Bizzie-Lizzie box. "I stole this from home this morning, and I've got to get it back in Lizzie's bedroom before she misses it."

Something between a laugh, a gasp and a yelp came out before Bobcat could stop it. "But how did you make it work?" he spluttered.

She held out her hand. On her palm lay one of the small sponges Mum used for putting on make-up. "Feel this."

He felt it. It was wet.

"I just held the sponge in my hand and touched it on the buzzer," explained Dandelion. "You can take the box off the blanket and attach it to Lizzie's underclothes, you know. It works just as well. So I climbed the wall bars, and got near you, and they never knew the difference."

"But we've got the trophy under false pretences!" protested Bobcat, recovering from his astonishment. "I should be disqualified."

"I only used it on the last run." She put the sponge in the pocket of her shorts. "On the first two you did it yourself."

He wasn't sure he had. "But what about Matt?"

She raised her eyebrows. "He was nowhere near the buzzer! You couldn't see him, but I watched him all the time. When you reached out to buzz, I just made sure you *did* buzz, that's all."

They looked at each other for a long minute. Bobcat struggled with his conscience. He knew his would be the nerve which broke first, and it was.

"Are you sure you can get the buzzer back into Lizzie's room?" he asked. "I'll help you if you like."

"No, thanks. I can do it." She smiled widely. "And thanks for not telling."

"Well," he admitted reluctantly. "You never tell on me."

BOBCAT AND THE PRETENDER TO THE THRONE

Samantha's friendship with Dandelion had died.

Within minutes of Dandelion's being chosen as carnival princess, Samantha's jealousy had killed it. She and her loyal followers – only Verity and one other now – never missed a chance to be nasty to Dandelion. And as the day of the Bash got nearer, they got nastier.

"What's that disgusting smell?" Samantha asked loudly as Bobcat and Dandelion came into the classroom the morning after the indoor sports. "You know what happens if you pick a dandelion, don't you, Catterick?"

There was some nervous giggling from Verity, but no one else joined in. Bobcat sat down at his table, trying to avoid sitting on the bruise he'd got when he'd fallen off the rope. He looked at the assorted faces of his classmates.

On the outside, things were still the same. They laughed at Dandelion's antics just like they'd always done. They still thought she was a fool with a funny name. But on the inside, something had changed. They'd voted her carnival princess. Bobcat knew this was partly to keep Samantha out, and partly because it was such a good opportunity to tease Dandelion about her make-believe princess. But he also knew that without consulting each other, and without knowing anything about what had happened to her before she came to Kneshworth, they'd all decided the same thing. For some reason, they were on Dandelion's side.

She beamed at Samantha. "You said you wanted to be my best friend. So *you* picked me first, didn't you?"

It was like that first morning, when she'd told Sir that he'd been rude. The whole class roared. With dignity, she sat down. "Have you seen my princess dress?" she asked Samantha in her clear, trembling voice. "It's *lovely*."

Of course Samantha had seen the dress. She'd been waiting all her life to wear it. "Shut up, Gardener," she snapped sulkily. "What does it matter how lovely it is? You'd look poo-awful in anything."

When the lunch bell went, Bobcat didn't go outside. He tossed the football to Joe and told him he'd catch him up. "Got something to do," he explained. "In the library."

"The *library*?" Joe twitched his glasses up his nose.

"Yeah, yeah. See you on the field."

Dandelion was already waiting beside the computer. Bobcat sat down and called up Tarantula. Then he tried **SUNFLOWER**. The screen didn't change.

"Rats!" he said.

"Rats? What have rats got to do with it?"

He sighed. "Nothing. I was just saying rats. You know."

"I hope there are no rats in the tower where my mother is," she murmured.

Here we go, thought Bobcat. "If you don't know where she is, how do you know she's in a tower?"

"Don't you know anything? Princesses are always imprisoned in towers." She frowned at the screen. "Let's try something else. How about Mural?"

Bobcat tried it. Nothing.

"Say the clue to me again," demanded Dandelion.

Feeling self-conscious, he said it. *"I creep to the sky, I follow the hours, Turning my face to the passing of time. Bewitched by my beauty? Then come with me, For the spell will lead you to clue number three."*

"It's not just the sunflowers," said Dandelion thoughtfully. "It's something else about that day. It's like the cricket match. It's

106

something to do with *you*, not me." Her eyes questioned him. "What did you do that afternoon?"

"I watched the presentation, just like everyone else."

"And then?"

"And then you jumped out of the mural, and all hell broke loose."

"And then?"

"And then I started shouting at you, and Samantha and Verity attacked me, and you and I ended up in Mrs Goodman's office." He screwed up his face at the thought. "Why am I telling you all this? You were there."

"It's important to think of everything that happened," she urged. "You might remember something I've forgotten. The password's in there somewhere, if only we can find it. Think!"

He tried hard to remember every detail he could. He tried **SAMANTHA** and **VERITY** and **GOODMAN** and **WINSTANLEY**. He even tried **JUNGLE**.

Nothing. Ten minutes had gone by and they'd got nowhere. And Ollie was at the door. "Come on, you lazy git, are you playing or not?"

"We'll have to leave it, Dandelion," Bobcat told her. "We'll do it later, on Dad's computer."

"Keep thinking," she instructed.

But no more possible passwords floated into his head the rest of that day, or the next. And then it was Saturday, the day of the Bash, and they still hadn't found the next clue.

"I've got rather a busy day today," Dandelion announced modestly, putting her head round Bobcat's bedroom door at eight o'clock, just as he was about to take his pyjama trousers off. "We'll have to leave the computer until tomorrow, if you don't mind."

"It's not *me* that minds. It's your game."

She stood there, not letting him get dressed. "I've got a rehearsal for the carnival parade this morning, and then the real thing at three o'clock. Will you come and watch me?"

"I suppose so. Dad'll be there with the video camera."

She clapped her hands. "Yippee! And just look at the weather! Oh, Bobcat, this is going to be the most perfect day ever!"

Bobcat thought she was probably right. During the morning the breeze died down and the sun brightened, clearing the cotton-woolly clouds from the sky. By the time Dandelion had come back from her rehearsal, eaten a sandwich and rushed off again to prepare for her three o'clock appearance, it was clear that it would be a perfect, still afternoon.

Mum, Dad, Lizzie and Bobcat gathered in the shade of the elm tree by the churchyard. Dad, the camera on his shoulder, wanted to get the best view of the start of the parade.

"Aren't you excited, children?" Bobcat thought Mum looked nice today, in jeans and a striped top. She looked young, and French, and pretty. She caught Dad's arm. "Martin – isn't that Peter Wood's truck?"

Melvin was trying to manoeuvre the balloon truck up the street to the school field, hampered by the spectators. Ollie's dad was leaning out of the passenger window, shouting at people to keep back if they didn't want their toes chopped off, and that balloon rides were a pound each, starting at half past four.

"That man!" hissed Mum. "Is he really going to take money off people to put their children in danger? Or did I not understand him?"

"You understood all right," said Dad. His hair flapped round his face, and he pushed it back with large, flat, gardening-scarred hands. "But he's a nice enough chap, even if he's a bit of a madman. And the money's for charity."

"It's all right, Dad, about the balloon..." began Bobcat.

"You're not going in that thing, and that's my final word," said Mum.

"Better do what the boss says," shrugged Dad.

It was five past three. "The band should have started by now," murmured Mum.

By ten past, people had begun to look at

their watches and mutter about useless organization, and say that they could do better themselves. Then a cheer went up as the first notes of brass instruments sounded.

"Pick me up!" Lizzie scrambled into Mum's arms. "I want to see Dandelion!"

The band marched round the corner of the church. As it passed by, the float with the carnival princess and her handmaidens on it came into view.

Bobcat was stunned. On the float were three chairs, but only two girls. In the carnival princess's chair, wearing the silver and white dress and the golden crown, sat Samantha Pilkington. Beside her, in one of the handmaidens' chairs, Verity Simmonds tried to look as if she hadn't been recently crying. The other chair was empty.

Dandelion simply wasn't there.

"Where's Dandelion?" asked Lizzie in dismay. "She told me she was going to be the princess!" Her voice rose to a wail. "She told me she'd wave to me!"

Bobcat saw shock on Mum's face, and disbelief on Dad's. Lizzie burst into tears.

"Where is she?" asked Mum. "What's that blonde girl doing there?" She turned to Dad, her face stiffening. "What's happened?"

"I brought her to the village hall at half past two," declared Dad. "I left her at the door, and she ran in. She must still be there."

"Come on." Mum put Lizzie down, took her hand and began to edge through the crowd.

Something cold had taken hold of Bobcat's insides, though he followed obediently. He didn't think Dandelion would be in the village hall.

She wasn't. A flustered woman explained that she just hadn't turned up. No one had seen her. "Samantha, bless her, volunteered to take her place, or we shouldn't have had a carnival princess at all!"

"But didn't you wonder where she was?" asked Dad, frowning.

"Yes, of course." She tossed her head, pretending not to notice Dad's concern. "But we assumed she'd changed her mind. Nerves, probably. She doesn't really belong here, you know. She's someone's foster-child, I believe."

Before Mum could speak Dad put his arm around her shoulders and pulled her away. "No one's going to help us here, Paul, so there's no point in making a fuss. You take the camera home and stay with Lizzie. Bob and I can look for her."

Mum looked very serious. She said something in French to Dad, who nodded, rubbing his hands together like he did before he started hauling boulders about people's gardens. "And we'll find her, won't we?" he said to Bobcat. "Let's try the school first."

They set off. Trying to keep pace beside Dad's strides, Bobcat considered miserably what might have happened.

First, Dandelion could have gone away of her own accord. But she was so happy and excited, he knew in his heart that she hadn't.

Second, someone could have taken her away. That was always a danger for any child, as Mum and Dad had repeatedly told him. Had they told Dandelion the same thing?

Third, she had injured herself in some way, and couldn't get help. Bobcat remembered something on TV about a girl who'd been out all night in winter on remote moorland after she twisted her ankle. But Kneshworth village on the busiest Saturday of the year wasn't remote moorland. And although Dandelion was only wearing a short skirt and a cotton top, it was a fine day in May. She couldn't possibly be in that kind of danger.

So what kind of danger *was* she in? He was sure that the only thing which could have kept her off the carnival princess's throne was foul play of some kind. His insides froze further. How could he explain this to Dad? And if he did, would it do any good, or merely worry him more?

"Hey, Bobcat!"

Joe and Ollie, wearing baseball caps and grinning, hurried towards him across the school field. Bobcat saw that Joe's borrowed

Liverpool strip was too big, with the shorts flapping about his skinny legs, but he hadn't the heart even to say, "Stylish!"

"Listen, Bobcat." Dad's face showed he'd had an idea. "Why don't you get Ollie and Joe to help you search the school and the field, while I head off into the village, and the farm? We can do it quicker if we split up. Meet you back here in half an hour."

"What's up?" said Joe as Dad departed. "Who are we looking for?"

"Dandelion."

"*Dandelion?*" Ollie stuck his hands in the pockets of his jeans and frowned impatiently. "But she's on the float, isn't she?"

"That's just it," explained Bobcat. "She *isn't* on the float. Samantha's sitting on the princess's throne, and the woman at the village hall says she hasn't seen Dandelion, even though Dad says he watched her go in the door at half past two. My parents are pretty worried."

Joe whistled softly. "I bet they are." He looked across the field to the school buildings. "Do you think she's in there?"

"I don't know. She might be hiding somewhere, I suppose."

"She's nutty enough to do anything," muttered Ollie.

Joe and Bobcat, who knew he was right, didn't reply.

The school was open on this special Saturday. Displays of competition entries were arranged in the hall, and covered the classroom walls. Later on, excited children would drag their parents round, eager to show off their work.

For now, though, the buildings were empty. Everyone was at the parade, or out on the field setting up stalls and hanging up bunting. Bobcat, Ollie and Joe opened every door except the cleaner's cupboard, which was locked. It had a window, though, which they looked through from the outside. There was no sign of Dandelion.

They sat down despondently at the edge of the field. "How long before your parents call the police?" asked Joe.

"When they're sure she isn't anywhere in the village," replied Bobcat. "By the end of the afternoon, I suppose."

"Before nightfall, then."

"Yes."

They all thought about Dandelion being out after nightfall. Into Bobcat's mind came a picture of rows of policemen searching the fields around the village, and divers emerging from the river. He'd seen it on TV. It was awful.

"I think something's happened to her," he said. "I mean, I can't say this to Dad, but I think someone's taken her away."

This took a minute to sink in. Then Joe

spoke, in a whisper. "Kidnapped her, you mean?"

Bobcat nodded.

"But who would do that?" asked Ollie.

"Someone who didn't want her to be on that float," said Bobcat.

Joe's head whipped round. "Someone who wishes she was the carnival princess herself, and thinks she should have been!"

In any other circumstances Bobcat would have laughed at the triumph on Joe's face and the bewilderment on Ollie's. "Exactly," he said to Joe. "The pretender to the throne – who else?"

"I wouldn't put anything past Samantha Pilkington," agreed Joe, nodding. "What do you think she's done with her?"

Ollie had cottoned on, but couldn't take it seriously. "She's probably chopped her into a thousand pieces and put her down a well!" he jeered. "Or perhaps she's dressed her up as a boy and sold her to pirates!"

"All right, Ollie." Joe turned to Bobcat, his face wearing its sensible look. "It's true, though. She must be hidden somewhere in the village."

"Had any luck, boys?" Dad walked quickly across the field. He could see as soon as he joined them that they hadn't. His face looked hot. His sweatshirt was tied round his waist. "Never mind. We'll split up again, shall we?

I haven't been to the farm yet."

None of the boys mentioned Samantha. It was obvious that they had to rescue Dandelion and return her safely to Dad without any grown-ups knowing what had happened.

"Don't worry, boys, we'll find her," said Dad. "She can't be far away."

All of a sudden, Bobcat found himself wondering just how far away she *could* be. He couldn't ignore the insane notion which had come to him.

Perhaps, despite all his scorn, it was possible that Dandelion's fantasy wasn't a fantasy after all. She might not be in a thousand pieces at the bottom of a well, or on a pirate ship, but could she have gone as far away as Harmon Major and All Its Dominions?

DANDELION AND THE RIGHTFUL HEIRESS

The parade had finished. Crowds were streaming in the school gates. The brass band was settling itself on the little bandstand in the shade, and people had begun to buy cups of tea and wander among the stalls. The balloon was tethered to the trees on the far side of the football pitch, waiting for its first passengers.

Neither the substitute carnival princess nor her handmaiden was anywhere to be seen. Their float stood forlornly on the road, looking less like a royal throne-room and more like a small lorry. Bobcat, Ollie and Joe gazed at it glumly.

"They've scarpered," concluded Ollie.

"We can see that." Joe scratched his head through his cap.

"Maybe they've gone to get Dandelion, now the parade's over," suggested Ollie. "Maybe she'll turn up at any moment."

"Oh, yeah. And she'll just come in quietly, and not tell anyone who kidnapped her," said Joe. "Think, Ollie. They've got to keep her wherever she is, and persuade her that telling on them is a *very* bad idea."

This hadn't occurred to Bobcat. "You mean they'll hurt her?"

"Of course they will. You said yourself that you wouldn't put anything past Samantha Pilkington."

Bobcat's heart began to beat faster. The imprisoned princess, tortured in the tower. And just like in fairy stories, someone had to rescue her, and restore the rightful heiress. Dandelion's fantasy was turning into reality, right here before his eyes.

"We've got to find her," he told Joe and Ollie. "We've got to find her as soon as we can."

"How?" asked Ollie. He looked truly anxious. "Where do we begin to look?"

It was then that Bobcat had an idea so blinding it cancelled out every other thought in his head. "Come on," he insisted, pulling Joe's T-shirt.

Joe and Ollie had no choice but to dash with him to the library. They pushed the door open and stumbled inside. "I've got to find the next clue," mumbled Bobcat, reaching for the computer switch.

"What are you talking about?" Joe sat down in the other computer chair, where

Dandelion had sat that day when the first clue had appeared. It seemed very long ago.

"Tarantula," said Bobcat. "It's a game. It's definitely on this machine, I've played it before. Come on, come *on*," he pleaded with the not yet started-up computer.

Joe and Ollie were staring at Bobcat as if he'd just got off a spaceship.

"There's no game called Tarantula," said Joe. He took off his hat and ran his fingers over his damp forehead. "I know. I read all the magazines." He gave Bobcat a straight, steady look. "Have you gone nuts or something?"

"And why do you want to play it *now*?" put in Ollie. "Aren't we supposed to be looking for Dandelion?"

"We *are* looking for Dandelion," insisted Bobcat. At last the computer was ready. "If I can find the answer to this clue, it might tell us where she is. It's just a guess, but I think it might work."

"I don't see how it can. There's no such game, I tell you." Joe was rolling and unrolling his cap between his hands. He looked unhappy. "And what's all this about clues?"

Bobcat sat back and took a deep breath. He'd never intended to tell Ollie and Joe, but this was an emergency. "According to Dandelion, the clues in the game are coded messages."

Two pairs of eyes met his in disbelief.

"Remember her story about her mother being a princess?" he asked them earnestly. "Well, she's playing a game where she pretends that her mother is imprisoned in a make-believe place, in another dimension, I suppose."

"Like the place in that book where they go through the wardrobe, and it's all snowing, and time stands still?" suggested Ollie, his eyes getting even rounder. "I liked the lion best in that. What happens is—"

"We know what happens," said Joe impatiently. "Go on, Bobcat. Where did Dandelion get these clues from?"

"From this computer. It's a game called Tarantula, like I told you."

"And like I told *you*," said Joe, "there's no such game."

"Maybe it's not called that, then. I don't know." Bobcat thought for a moment. "But whatever it's called, Dandelion and I couldn't find the first clue until we typed in the correct password."

Joe and Ollie were interested. "What was the password?" asked Ollie.

"I can't remember," lied Bobcat. It would be too embarrassing, explaining the stuff about King of the Sixers. "But anyway, Dandelion says that the answer to each clue is the password into the next. We solved the first clue, and we've nearly solved the second.

That's what I want to do now, so I can get the third clue."

He waited while Ollie and Joe digested this information. "But why do you want to get the third clue?" asked Joe.

"Because I think it'll lead us to Dandelion."

Joe frowned. Bobcat could almost see his brain ticking over. "But the clues are supposed to tell you where the *princess* is, not Dandelion."

"Exactly!" Bobcat almost shouted. "And what was Dandelion supposed to be today?"

They didn't say anything.

"Don't you understand?" asked Bobcat, looking from Ollie to Joe and back again. "*Dandelion's* the princess who's been taken away and imprisoned, just like in her fantasy!"

They still looked blank. "But it's all crazy!" cried Ollie. "It's just a girls' story, about princesses and knights on horses with swords. What's it got to do with computers? And why are you taking it so seriously? You're just a git, aren't you, Catterick?"

"Because the game's *not* crazy," explained Bobcat. "Every clue has something to do with real life, real things happening. The one we've been trying to get is something to do with that mural in the playground. The one before was about the cricket match. Believe me, the next one will be about something here, right now." He typed TARANTULA. For a moment he feared it wouldn't work without Dandelion

121

being there, but the screen darkened and the spider with the green eyes appeared. "See?" he said triumphantly. "It *is* here!"

"Well, I've never seen it before," muttered Joe. "What now?"

"I've already tried all the obvious words about the mural," said Bobcat. "It's got to be something about *me*, Dandelion says. Can you remember anything *I* did that day?"

They thought. "You were in a fight with those two witches," said Joe. "If I hadn't come along and rescued you—"

"Joe!" Bobcat's fingers flew over the keys. He typed in RESCUE. "Press Enter" said the screen.

The ENTER key filled the screen with silver light. When it had cleared, and Ollie and Joe had taken their hands away from their eyes, the three boys read the clue.

Don't fly too near the tops of
   the trees,
Which guard the fields by night
   and day.
Keep your head, fall to your
   knees,
And bear me safely, silently away.

"By Jupiter," breathed Bobcat softly. "It's the balloon."

*   *   *

Later, when Bobcat tried to answer questions about what happened, he found he couldn't remember how he, Ollie and Joe got from the library to the field where the balloon was tethered. He supposed they must have run, but he couldn't picture them doing it. All he knew was that they had to get to Dandelion before Samantha did.

The balloon basket was still empty. It was tethered by three long ropes, two attached to trees, and one to the back of the truck. Ollie had explained to Bobcat what happened in a tethered balloon ride. When the truck drove a few yards down the field, the ropes would extend and the balloon would rise up. Then, when the ride was over, the pilot would turn off the burner, the truck would drive back and the balloon would land, ready for the next group of passengers.

Melvin was knocking a sign saying BALLOON RIDES, £1 into the grass with a mallet, while Ollie's dad supervised the line of excited children. "Only three children or two adults at a time," he was saying. "Cheap at twice the price. All proceeds to charity."

"Where are we going?" asked one of the children, a girl, shouting above the roar of the fan.

"Where the wind blows us, m'darling," said Melvin cheerfully, kicking the post the sign was nailed to. He put down the mallet and wiped his upper lip with the back of his hand. "About thirty feet up," he explained to the girl's mother.

Bobcat looked breathlessly at his watch. Twenty-three minutes past four. The first ride was due at half past. The basket still lay on its side, though the balloon was already almost completely inflated. Any minute now, Ollie's dad would start the burner and climb inside the upright basket, and Melvin would lift three children over the sides.

"Come on, you two!" he called. "Dandelion must be hidden in the basket! Quick!"

It was Samantha's blue headband which gave her away. As Bobcat and the other boys ran towards the balloon, a flash of blue bobbed up from its hiding-place behind the truck. She had unclipped the two tree-ropes.

Bobcat knew what she was going to do next.

"No!" he shrieked. "Samantha! Stop!"

But it was too late. She detached the third rope from the truck. Bobcat watched in horror as the basket skidded into the upright position.

"Hey!" Melvin came running. "What are you kids up to?"

Bobcat tore blindly towards the basket, his feet slipping on the flattened grass. But before he got there, Ollie's dad had pulled the red lever which operated the burner. The basket skidded again.

He grabbed Ollie's dad's arm. "You've got to stop it!" he urged, as the basket tilted dangerously, then began to lift off the ground. "The ropes are untied!"

"*What?*" Ollie's dad's face changed. He turned the burner off. "For God's sake tie them up again, then!" he called. "I'll try to bring it down!"

He grabbed a rope looped on the outside of the basket and swung his leg up, trying to climb in. But it was too late. The basket was already too far off the ground. He gave a cry and fell off.

Relieved of his weight, the basket rose like a rocket into the sky. Bobcat's heart was bursting in his chest. His voice wouldn't come out properly. "She's in there!" he shouted above all the other noise, but no one heard him.

Without the ropes, the hot air inside the balloon would make it float away. Without a pilot. Out of control. Taking Dandelion helplessly away like the clue said. Too near the river, too near the tops of the trees.

Melvin and Ollie's dad, bellowing at people to get out of the way, caught at the loose ropes that flailed around the drunken balloon. Melvin, who had locked Samantha in the cab, hung onto the truck-rope with all his weight. But the volume of hot air in the enormous balloon was too big for anyone to tackle single-handed.

In a flash Bobcat knew what he had to do. He kicked off his slippery-soled trainers and peeled off his socks. He spat on his hands and smeared the spit between his palms. He pulled Melvin's torn T-shirt.

Melvin was very annoyed. "Clear off!" he shouted. "Haven't you stupid kids caused enough trouble yet? This balloon's worth thousands. If we don't get it back—"

"I'll get it back!" Bobcat assured him. "Just give me the rope!"

"What the hell do you think you're going to do? Climb it?"

"Just watch me." Bobcat grabbed the rope.

"Hey!" shouted Melvin, and lunged at Bobcat. But Bobcat was lighter, and much quicker, and dodged out of his way.

Climbing the rope was a lot harder than climbing the ropes in the school hall. It was thick, and coarse, and rubbed painfully against Bobcat's legs even through his knee-length shorts. And instead of ending in a solid ceiling beam, this rope was wild. It writhed like a snake, whipped by a gravity-denying force which almost pulled Bobcat's arms out of their sockets.

He climbed on, gripping the rope sturdily with his bare feet. Below him, everyone had stopped shouting. Bobcat was dimly aware that if his strength failed him this time, there was no pile of mats and no Sir to break his fall.

The only way to go was up, into the basket. Once there, he could only hope that something – he didn't even know what – would bring the balloon down.

He tried not to panic. He tried not to think about the balloon landing. He tried not to think about tomorrow's blisters. He kept his head up and looked at the sky so that he didn't have to look at the ground. The brass band was still playing. The sound seemed very far away. Just another few centimetres, and another few...

When he reached the basket a cheer went up, but Bobcat hardly heard it. His hands and feet smarting, he grasped the edge, slung one leg over it, almost lost his balance, cried out, and tumbled in.

There was no sign of Dandelion, but Bobcat could hear a whimpering sound coming from the large canvas bag used for storing the balloon when it wasn't in use, which lay along one side of the basket. The canvas was tough, and tightly rolled, but he wrenched it open.

She was lying there, her arms and legs crumpled up uncomfortably. Over her mouth was a piece of sticking-plaster. Her hands and feet were tied with brightly coloured headscarves. Bobcat almost wanted to laugh, she looked so exactly like kidnap victims are supposed to look. But he felt sorry for her. How long had she been there, invisible, unheard, hardly able

to breathe, wondering if she would ever be rescued? How long ago – two hours at least – had
Samantha lured her there?

He eased the sticking-plaster away from her
lips. She began to cry. Tears trickled across the
bridge of her nose, into her ear. She stayed on
the floor of the basket, breathing heavily
through her mouth, her eyes closed. He wondered if she knew the danger she was in. On
the whole, he hoped she didn't.

The balloon dipped suddenly, throwing
Bobcat against the side of the basket. Warily,
he looked over the edge. The crowd had
grown. In the middle of it, he saw with a jolt,
was Mum's striped jumper and horrified face.
"Robert! Robert!" she was shrieking. "Come
down at *once*!"

"I'm trying to!" he called back.

There was some laughter, but Ollie's dad's
voice rang out seriously. "Bobcat, listen to me.
You are responsible for many thousands of
pounds' worth of equipment. Do you hear me?"

"Yes."

"Ollie says your sister's in there too. Is that
true?"

"Yes." There was no point in telling him she
wasn't his sister.

"Is she all right?"

"Yes."

"Are you a brave boy?"

"No!" wailed Mum.

"I hope so," said Bobcat.

"I want you to start the burner," instructed Ollie's dad. "The hot air level's dropping fast and if it drops any more you'll have a crash landing. You've got to keep the air hot until we've secured the ropes. Do you understand?"

"Yes."

"Pull the red lever until I tell you to push it up again." He raised his right arm. "I'll signal by dropping my arm."

Bobcat could see what he was trying to do. He pulled the red handle. The basket tilted alarmingly. Bobcat grabbed a metal bar which seemed to be there for the purpose, and hung on. At last Ollie's dad's arm came down, and Bobcat pushed the handle up again with all his strength. Gripping the side of the basket, he peeped over. Dad and Ollie's dad and Melvin all gave him a thumbs-up sign.

"Great stuff!" said Melvin.

"Can you get Dandelion up?" called Dad. "Peter wants you both to stand up and brace yourselves against the sides of the basket. Hold on tight, or you might get thrown out."

Bobcat untied Dandelion's wrists, and she untied her feet herself.

"My legs hurt," she said. "And I'm so thirsty!"

"Can you get out of there and stand up?"

"I'm scared, Bobcat."

"It's all right. Stand up."

He hauled her out of the canvas bag onto her feet. It wasn't like lifting Lizzie. Though Dandelion was thin, she was tall. Pain shot up both his arms. "Hang onto these loops on the inside of the basket," he instructed. "And don't look down."

They stood in different corners. The balloon was only a little higher than the treetops, but the ground looked miles away. For the first time Bobcat began to feel frightened.

"I'm cold," said Dandelion miserably. It wasn't cold – the late afternoon sunshine and the still air were perfect for ballooning, in fact – but Dandelion was shivering, and fright had raised goose bumps on her arms. "What's happening?"

"They're trying to pull the basket down. Hold on tight." He peered over. Ollie was hanging on the end of one of the ropes, swaying backwards and forwards like a parrot on a perch. "This is fun!" Bobcat heard him cry before his father yanked the rope out of his hands.

Within a couple of minutes all the ropes were secured. But the basket pitched sideways, towards the parked truck. Bobcat saw Samantha, still imprisoned in the cab, put her hands to her face in alarm. One of the bottom corners of the basket clipped the roof of the cab. The impact threw Dandelion to the floor. She landed on her bare knees, yelping in pain.

Then the basket hit the grass, and fell on its side.

It was all over. As he and Dandelion crawled out, Bobcat realized he'd collected some bruises to add to the blisters. He sat on the grass. His watch told him that only four and a half minutes had passed since he'd last looked at the time. He couldn't – he just *couldn't* – believe it.

Dandelion was crying, Lizzie was crying, Mum was crying. Dad knelt down beside Bobcat and held him to his chest for a long time. Bobcat didn't feel like crying, though. He didn't feel like anything. He thought vaguely about Samantha, whose mum was also crying, and whose dad was exchanging words with Ollie's dad. Mostly, though, he thought about the clue.

He was pretty sure it contained the words, *Keep your head, fall to your knees*. He'd done the first thing, and Dandelion the second. But the balloon wasn't bearing anyone safely, silently away. The basket was just lying there, with Melvin trying to clear people off the place on the field where the deflating balloon was about to fall. Maybe…

"Come on, let's go home," said Dad, releasing him.

He took Lizzie's hand, and Mum took Dandelion's, and they walked towards the school gate.

Maybe, thought Bobcat, the last part of the clue hasn't come true yet.

Miss Waller put her briefcase on the kitchen table and smiled brightly.

"Cake?" Mum offered the plate, but Miss Waller refused.

"Just coffee for me, thank you, Mrs Catterick. Black, one sugar."

Dandelion, Bobcat and Lizzie watched while she took two sips of coffee without wetting her lipsticked lips. "Real French coffee!" she said, smiling even wider. "Delicious!" She put down the cup. "However, I didn't come here just to drink delicious coffee."

She flipped open the top of the briefcase and took out a pale green folder. "Do you know what this is, Dandelion?"

"It's a cardboard folder," warbled Dandelion.

"Of course it is, dear," said Miss Waller. "But it's got something very special inside it."

"Is it a present?" asked Dandelion. Dad, who was standing behind Dandelion's chair, squeezed her shoulder gently.

Miss Waller moved the cake plate aside and spread some papers on the table. She laid a pink-varnished fingernail on one of them. "This is a letter we received a week ago, from France."

"Is it in French?" asked Dandelion eagerly.

"Mum'll translate it, won't you, Mum?"

"No, it's not in French." Miss Waller's pink nail moved to the other piece of paper. "And this is a special form which Mr and Mrs Catterick are going to sign. Then I can take the next step."

"The next step where?" asked Dandelion.

Miss Waller picked up the letter. "This letter is addressed to me, from a hospital in Paris," she announced. "It says that Madame Azalie Gardener – that's your mother, Dandelion – has left the hospital and is living with her parents – that's your grandparents – while she awaits the arrival of her daughter from England."

"That's me," said Dandelion.

Everyone laughed, and looked at Dandelion. She had an expression on her face which Bobcat had often seen. Excited, but in control.

"Is she the princess?" asked Lizzie.

Miss Waller gazed at her with brown, wide-set eyes. "Yes, Lizzie, she's the princess." She flicked a tiny look at Mum, who shook her head and put her finger lightly to her lips.

Dandelion whispered to Bobcat, "You see? It's just like I told you. The rightful heiress is back. And it's *you* who led me to her."

Miss Waller smiled fondly at Dandelion. "You can join her as soon as the forms are signed." She leaned across the table. "Isn't it exciting?"

Dandelion's eyes shone with a polished-pewter gleam. The light from the kitchen window made a bright border round her yellow hair. It was only a month since she'd arrived, but Bobcat no longer thought she looked odd. She just looked like Dandelion.

Dad was still holding her shoulder. "You'll like living in Paris with your grandparents, won't you?" he asked, smiling.

"Of course!" She took Dad's hand, then turned back to Miss Waller. "But why have I never seen them?"

"Because your mother quarrelled with them years ago, when she and your father got married and she came to live in England," explained Miss Waller. "They wanted her to marry someone else."

"I've never seen my father either!" exclaimed Dandelion. She was holding Dad's hand very tightly. "What happened to him?"

"We don't know," said Miss Waller solemnly. "When you were a baby he disappeared. Your mother couldn't take you back to France because her family disapproved of her marriage. But when you were still quite little – about Lizzie's age – she became ill, and had to go to a special hospital. That's when you were taken into our care."

Mum had noticed Bobcat's concern. "When Dad and I applied to be foster-parents," she explained to him, "Miss Waller sent her to us because I'm French. We thought it might help, though we weren't sure she'd even remember her own mother."

"I *do* remember her," said Dandelion decisively. "I remember how pretty she was, and her blonde hair, and the lovely clothes she used to wear." Tears sparkled in the corners of her eyes, but didn't fall. "She used to tell me about Princess Azalea, Crown Princess of Harmon Major and All Its Dominions. She said the princess couldn't go back because she'd made some enemies."

Something occurred to Bobcat, but he didn't say it.

"Anyway," said Miss Waller, "when they discovered she was ill they forgave her, and took her back to France. They asked us to go on looking after Dandelion until they were sure their daughter's condition would improve." She gave Dandelion an encouraging look. "And now it has. She's much better, and she's waiting for you."

Mum hugged Dandelion. "It's been lovely having you here with us, but you belong with your own mother, who loves you."

"Do you think she loves me?" asked Dandelion.

"But of course!" Mum's French accent thickened. "And your grandparents will love you too, when they get to know you. Just like we do."

Miss Waller picked up the form which still lay on the table. "This form is the next step, Dandelion," she said softly. "When Mr and Mrs Catterick sign it, it will mean you are released from their care. When your mother signs another form you will be in her care again. Do you understand?"

Lizzie burst into tears. "I don't want Dandelion to go away!"

"None of us do," said Dad. "But you're a big girl, Liz. You can write her a letter, can't you?" He picked Lizzie up so that she could see out of the window. "Now, who's this?"

Someone had opened the back gate and was coming up the garden. It was Ollie. "Ready, Bobcat?" he called through the open door.

"Ready for what?"

Everyone was looking at Bobcat. "Ready for *what*?" he repeated.

"It's a present from Mum," said Dandelion. "For rescuing me."

"Come on, or we'll go without you," clamoured Ollie. "Joe's already in the car. Look, you can see the balloon from here."

A smiling Melvin delivered the three boys to the farm field at the edge of the village. Ollie's dad, already in the basket, helped them scramble over the sides. The burner roared, and the basket soared upwards so terrifyingly swiftly that Bobcat's breath disappeared. Joe was shouting, but Bobcat couldn't hear him.

Once they were up, all was calm. Apart from occasional noises from the ground – the throb of a combine harvester, a train rattling over the level-crossing – the balloon floated in a safe, silent world, just like the clue said. People shaded their eyes and waved, and the boys waved back. As they drifted on, Bobcat leaned dreamily against the side of the basket, thinking.

He thought about Tarantula. Whatever Joe said, it must be a game. The clues were fun, but they weren't anything to do with Dandelion's mother. They just happened to coincide with real events. Just like Dandelion's predictions happened to come true. Perhaps, he reasoned, if you convince yourself hard enough that something's going to happen, it does.

He thought about the invisible line between the real world and the world of make-believe. Long before she came to live with them, Dandelion had crossed that line and then not known how to get back. She'd actually started to believe her fantasy. And for a moment, for a split second on that dreadful afternoon, he'd believed it too. Just like Dandelion, he'd discovered it was sometimes easier to believe a fantasy than face the truth.

Joe's voice broke into his thoughts. "Guess what I did yesterday."

"What?"

"I tried to get into Tarantula again. I mean,

it looked a fun game."

Bobcat heard the doubt in Joe's tone. "And what happened?"

"Nothing."

The wind blew Bobcat's hair into his eyes. He pulled his cap from his pocket and put it on. "What do you mean, nothing?"

"The game doesn't exist. I was right all along."

"But it existed on Saturday afternoon!" protested Bobcat. "You saw it!" He turned to Ollie. "And so did you!"

Ollie shrugged. "If you really want to know what I think, Catterick, I think—"

"I know," sighed Bobcat. "I'm a git."

The balloon was getting higher. The air was cooler, though the sun was very bright. Bobcat was glad he was wearing a sweatshirt. He drew his cap further down over his forehead and gazed at the horizon. A silver streak, far away between the land and the sky, was the sea. The English Channel. And even further away, on the other side, was France. The country which had invented ballooning, which had given him Mum, and which would take Dandelion to its heart.

A thought struck him with such violence that he staggered, and Ollie had to haul him upright again. He began to laugh. He laughed so much that he felt weak, and had to clutch his stomach.

"What's the joke?" demanded Joe.

Bobcat laughed some more. "That's just it, it's a joke! About picking a dandelion and wetting the bed!"

"Not *that* again!" Ollie scowled at him crossly. "It isn't even funny."

"Yes it is," he said, between chuckles. "I mean, Dandelion's going to be living in France!"

"So why's that funny?" asked Joe.

Bobcat was too weak to stand. He slid down the side of the basket and sat on the floor, giggling and snorting, looking up at their baffled faces.

"Wait until after Dandelion's gone," he suggested, "so that she doesn't beat you up. Then ask my mum the French word for dandelion!"

UNDERCOVER ANGEL

Dyan Sheldon

Twelve-year-old Elmo Blue admires his neighbours, the Bambers – they're so nice and normal. Not like Elmo's embarrassing mother, who is declaring war on Mr Bamber over his plans to turn the local woods into a golf course. Elmo pins his hopes of being normal on making friends with the Bambers' new adopted child, an orphan from South America. But when the kid arrives, claiming to be an undercover angel, Elmo realizes that in fact his life is going to become distinctly weirder!

"Another thoroughly good read from a reliably entertaining author." *Kids Out*

THE FRENCH CONFECTION

Anthony Horowitz

"Tim," I asked. "What's the French for 'murder'?"

Tim shrugged. "Why do you want to know?"

"I don't know." I stepped onto the escalator and let it carry me down. "I've just got a feeling it's something we're going to need."

When the hard-up Diamond brothers, Tim and Nick, win a weekend for two in Paris, it looks as if their luck is taking a turn for the better. But looks can be deceptive. No sooner have they arrived in the French capital than the brothers are up to their necks in danger. There's a nasty smell in the air and it's not the cheese. If Nick and Tim aren't careful, their dream holiday could end up being a nightmare from which they'll never wake…